"You've gone too far," he rasped

Cavan lowered his body onto hers, and she shrank into the mattress at the intensity of the heat burning through her, right through her clothes. He lifted her arms over her head and studied her face.

"Before I leave for my trip I have to seal this intolerable, painful, inescapable bond between us. If I don't, God knows what you'll do, where you'll go."

"You won't have the satisfaction of surrender."

"Oh, yes, I will," he said arrogantly. He kissed her sullen mouth, and she wrenched her head away, but it didn't matter to him that she was trying to avoid his touch. "But I don't think I'll get anywhere by forcing you. There are better ways," he said with a softly sensual satisfaction. His mouth searched warmly over her neck.

SARA WOOD spent her childhood in Portsmouth, which meant grubby knees and flying pigtails. She worked as a typist, seaside landlady and teacher until writing gave her the freedom her Romany blood craved. Happily married, she has two handsome sons; Richard is married and Simon is a roamer—always with beautiful girls. Sara lives in the Cornish countryside where her writing life alternates with her passion for gardening, which allows her to be grubby again!

Books by Sara Wood

SARA WOOD

Dark Forces

Harlequin Books

TORONTO • NEW YORK • LONDON
AMSTERDAM • PARIS • SYDNEY • HAMBURG
STOCKHOLM • ATHENS • TOKYO • MILAN
MADRID • WARSAW • BUDAPEST • AUCKLAND

ISBN 0-373-11606-3

DARK FORCES

Copyright © 1992 by Sara Wood.

This edition published by arrangement with Harlequin Enterprises B. V.

® and TM are trademarks of the publisher. Trademarks indicated with ® are registered in the United States Patent and Trademark Office, the Canadian Trade Marks Office and in other countries.

Printed in U.S.A.

CHAPTER ONE

'Mawgan! Stop the car!' Bethany leaned forwards, her cap of dark hair ruffling in the sea breeze. Her face relaxed into a pensive smile as she looked down on Portallen Bay.

'Gorgeous, isn't it?' said her brother smugly. 'Now don't you wish you'd come back sooner?'

From their vantage point on the headland, Bethany could see the sandy beach glistening in the September sun from the wash of the outgoing tide. 'How could I?' she asked quietly, her blue-grey eyes as dark as Cornish slate. 'I'd lost my nerve.' Her tongue touched her dry lips and she tasted the tang of salt. 'Heavens! I'm shaking like a leaf,' she confessed.

'I keep telling you,' he insisted. 'It's all blown over.'

'Really? They hated me so much...' Bethany's gaze drifted across the white crescent of sand to the jagged rocks where seams of rock crystal gleamed. The sun bounced off the sea, dazzling her, highlighting a beautiful ketch sailing around the headland. 'How lovely...I can't stay long,' she sighed sadly.

'I know. Just until we get the hotel back into shape. Poor Beth, it's been hard for you to return,' said Mawgan gently, squeezing her hand. 'I'm very grateful.'

'I'd do anything for you, you know that,' she said warmly, putting aside her anxiety. Mawgan needed her. 'You're all I have,' she added.

Her brother seemed about to say something, but changed his mind and fell silent. Bethany wished he'd chatter and stop her from wondering what lay ahead. It would be bad enough driving through the village in an open car and being stared at again. But there was something else that worried her more. Cavan.

Breathing deeply to calm her nerves, she inhaled the freshness of the emerald-green grass, the warmth of the sun-drenched soil, the rich smell of autumn. Bethany dragged her eyes from the humped hills rising above the deep river valley and the grazing sheep arranged artfully on their slopes, and tried to steer her mind away from her apprehensions.

'You haven't told me much about this disastrous re-fit you had done on the hotel,' she said briskly, being as practical as possible.

'There's a reason for that,' muttered Mawgan, starting up the car and beginning the steep plunge to the coast. 'I feel such a fool. Talk about fast-sell methods! The hotel needed modernising, and Cavan had only given me a small budget so I let this cheapjack firm go ahead. I hope you can salvage something out of the mess without much expense.'

'A bit of well-aimed drapery can hide a lot of faults,' soothed Bethany, wishing it would do the same for her. 'Are you sure I look all right?' she asked, her hands suddenly clammy with nerves. The village was in sight. She could see the stone fishermen's houses ahead, grey and severe.

'Fantastic. Like a film star,' said her brother.

'That's what I was afraid of,' she said wryly, checking her dark, glossy hair. The narrow tarmac road with grass running down the centre gave way to cobbles, and Mawgan gingerly manoeuvred his old Morris convertible at a bone-rattling crawl along the narrow street. Bethany steeled herself to withstand the intense curiosity her visit was arousing.

She knew everyone, and tried to smile in greeting. But the villagers remained unresponsive, their faces cold, unwelcoming. She felt crushed by their uninhibited stares as they inspected every inch of her from her neat, dark Sassoon bob, her huge gold earrings and necklace, the white linen suit with its tight and short sheath skirt, and the long length of slim, tanned thigh and leg, visible to anyone who peered into the well of the car.

And they did, shamelessly. As a daughter of Portallen, Bethany still belonged to them, and they assumed rights over her.

'I *knew* they'd bristle if I wore something glamorous,' she said unhappily to Mawgan.

'I wasn't having you returning cap in hand,' he said firmly. 'I'm proud of you. Chin up, we're almost home.'

He entered the lane which led to the hotel, and stopped in the courtyard. Bethany felt quite exhausted from tension. 'I don't want to do that again in a hurry,' she said shakily. 'They scrutinised me, right down to the labels on my underwear!'

'Silly! They were curious,' smiled Mawgan.

'Hostile,' she amended, worried whether she could cope. But her face relaxed into a smile as her hungry eyes examined every inch of the small medieval manor house which her father had turned into the village hotel. 'Home,' she breathed, clutching Mawgan's hand tightly. 'Home at last.'

Her brother stiffened. 'Oh, no!' he groaned. 'He said——'

Bethany followed his gaze and her face paled. In the side lane was parked a vibrant red Aston Martin. '*Cavan*!' she said in distress. Inside her, everything was jumping: her heart, her stomach, her pulses, her brain. 'What's he doing here? You said he hardly ever came here,' she reminded Mawgan, an accusing note in her voice. 'You said I wouldn't see him. You said——'

'Beth,' cut in Mawgan gently, 'he owns the hotel. He has a right to be here.'

'That's the trouble, isn't it?' she said bitterly, the resentment of years souring her voice. 'He owns it! I could just about stomach that, but he doesn't give a damn about it. I dread to think what he'll do with it eventually. I love Portallen.'

Upset and trembling, Bethany jerked down the handle of the car door. Her intended graceful exit was marred by the fact that the door was jammed. Before Mawgan could dart around to help her, a figure loomed up as if from nowhere and a strong hand wrenched the door open by sheer brute force.

'Love? You have a funny way of showing your love,' came Cavan's throaty growl.

Hiding her nervousness, Bethany slid out her long and suddenly alarmingly exposed legs to the ground, steadied herself on the spindly shoes and stood up, smoothing down her short skirt unnecessarily while she waited for the pulses in her body to stop leaping around like sprats in a net.

'Afternoon, Cavan,' she said evenly.

'Good afternoon, beautiful. Don't you have a kiss for your stepbrother?' he murmured.

His rough, gravelly voice reverberated through her body, sliding into every crevice in a warm and insistent flame. 'No, I don't,' she said firmly, reaching in the car for her bag. And still not meeting his eyes. She wasn't ready.

'Hi, Cavan,' said Mawgan with false cheerfulness, trying to prise the two from their mutual dislike. 'You look well.'

Cavan merely nodded in Mawgan's direction as if he wasn't important. Bethany held back her irritation. 'Perhaps you'd explain what you mean by saying I have a funny way of showing my love for Portallen,' she said haughtily.

He chuckled. 'Still proud, Bethany.' He blocked her way, his body as brawny as a wrestler's. Her sensory memories were instantly aroused as her nostrils were assailed by the fierce blood-heat emanating from him, mingled with the faint scent of *Pour les Hommes*—his aftershave. He'd been running, she mused. He was fired up with energy and panting slightly.

She needed time to get used to his arrival. Bethany fumbled in her bag. She brought out her compact and pretended to check her make-up.

'Yes,' he murmured softly. 'Still proud.'

'Could that be because I have a lot to be proud of?' she asked casually, snapping the compact shut. She continued to rummage in her bag and then it was closed for her by a large male hand.

'On the surface it would seem so. You're perfect,' mocked Cavan. 'Externally.'

He never lost an opportunity to hurt her, she frowned. Physical memories crowded in when he stepped closer— that body-disturbing magnetism and sexuality which was unique to Cavan flowing around her, making her throat dry up. Slowly she lifted her head. It had a long way to go. Although she was of average height, she'd almost forgotten how neck-cricking it could be to stare him out.

By the time she'd shaped her expression into haughty lines and met his wickedly crinkling ice-blue eyes with a scathing look, she'd had to cope with the sight of the daunting width of his gently heaving chest and tough-guy shoulders, giving the lie to the surprisingly conventional pin-stripe navy suit which had been expertly moulded to his strong body.

'Thank you,' she said, proud of her steady voice. 'Now explain that gibe you made, questioning the strength of my feelings about Portallen.'

'They seem a little...lacking in depth.' His mouth quirked in amusement at her cold stare. 'For someone who professes to adore the place, you sure high-tailed it out of here fast. Let's face it, you were only eighteen when you latched on to the first rich man who stayed at the hotel and shot off to get married in Scotland. Long way from Cornwall, Scotland.'

'His job was there. If you love someone, you...' She faltered. There was a dangerous, frightening light in Cavan's eyes suddenly, and she couldn't continue with what she'd been about to say. Stunned by the thinly veiled venom pouring out of him towards her, she blinked rapidly.

'If you love someone, you will follow them anywhere,' said Cavan softly, not sparing her.

She clenched her trembling hands. 'Exactly. Dan and I were in love,' she said tightly, frowning when he lifted a disbelieving eyebrow.

'Oh. We're talking about Dan, are we?' murmured Cavan.

'Haven't you got any sensitivity?' asked Bethany, dry-mouthed. 'I'd rather we didn't discuss my late husband. My first thought was to drive down from Aberdeen when he died so that I could be with people I knew, in a place I loved. And look where it got me,' she added bitterly.

'Dan died three years ago. You've been away for two,' said Cavan remorselessly. 'Living the high life, by the looks of you.' His scornful eyes skimmed her elegant suit. 'When you ran from this village because of that hate campaign, you vanished as if you'd gone from the face of the earth. God knows where you went, but I did think you'd come back after a while, even for a brief visit to your old haunts. I suppose you prefer city life now. More hairdressers. Fashion shops. Men.'

A wry smile touched her full mouth. If he knew! The picture he was painting was far from the truth. And her banishment from Portallen had been all his fault. Her eyes flickered like sparking flint when she realised that he was taunting her with the memories deliberately.

'You're trying to upset me. And failing,' she said coldly, wondering why Mawgan didn't protest on her behalf. 'You know perfectly well why I stayed away. Those poison-pen letters were vile.'

'Yes, the gossip was malicious, Cavan. Surely you remember,' interjected Mawgan, looking puzzled. 'For God's sake, Beth had just been widowed. She came here to grieve and within a short while she was being hounded by the very people she'd known since she was a kid. She was shunned and reviled by friends. Can you imagine that, Cavan? Beth's tough, but she was damned vulnerable at that time. The gossip all but destroyed her confidence.'

Cavan shrugged. 'They gossip about me constantly.'

'But you're thick-skinned,' Bethany said curtly. 'And you aren't bothered about what people think or you wouldn't have behaved so atrociously.'

'Are you referring to my dubious employment as a thuggish bouncer in Plymouth, or as a crooked ticket-tout in the East End?' he asked sarcastically.

Bethany tried to remain calm and keep her dignity. Cavan was throwing her own words back at her, and they sounded embarrassingly spiteful. 'I mean that outrageous assault on me in Fore Street,' she said stiffly. It rankled even now.

'Oh, that.' His eyes crinkled. 'You know, we'd startled the village often enough with our rows, but that was a classic,' he recalled with satisfaction. 'Better than a cabaret, wasn't it? There's still red paint on the wall where my old Ferrari wedged your car against the butcher's shop.'

'You humiliated me!' she said tightly.

'Did I?' It seemed as if his voice became huskier than ever. 'Because I hauled you out of the driver's seat and kissed you?' He thoughtfully stroked his cheek as if remembering her answering slap, and she flushed. Cavan brought out the worst in her. She never managed to keep her emotions under control when he was around—but then he *tormented* her so. 'Is your sense of honour satisfied or shall we stand back to back, take ten paces, turn and fire?' he asked in amusement, his teeth dazzling her for a moment.

She contemplated him thoughtfully, her heart pumping hard. 'I wouldn't dream of turning my back on you,' she said quietly. 'As for my honour, you might bear it in mind that I don't like being embarrassed in public or kissed by someone whom I dislike intensely.'

Cavan took her arms in his firm, possessive grip, his face suddenly serious. 'Bethany, I was trying to persuade you not to run away——'

'You liar!' she began with soft vehemence, and then stopped herself in time. She didn't want to get into an argument with Cavan. Or to reveal her suspicions. 'Mawgan, would you help me in with my things?' she asked her brother, letting warmth flood her voice, and hoping that Cavan would take note of the contrast in her manner.

'Good God!' cried Cavan, frowning. 'You're not planning on *staying* in the hotel, are you?'

To her alarm, he'd drawn her closer, as if she belonged to him, and she desperately wanted to beat him on the chest and escape. But he would have won, then.

'You can't object to me having my old room,' she said, apparently composed. Disdainfully she tried to pluck his fingers off and failed. He was no gentleman. She frowned at his hands. Once they'd been rough from manual work. Now they were smooth and beautifully manicured.

Cavan's eyes slid to Mawgan. 'Has she any idea of what's awaiting her?' he asked, his expression forbidding.

'What do you mean?' asked Bethany warily, glancing at the building. Frowning, she saw that there was something wrong with the windows, but she couldn't work out what it was. Suddenly alarmed, she turned her head quickly back to Cavan and clutched at his lapels. 'Who's in there?' she demanded huskily. 'The Men's Committee?' He didn't answer. His eyes were brooding on her, his face growing more sensual every second, and she became even more confused and agitated. 'The Women's Institute? They want me to leave?'

'Relax,' he murmured, taking the opportunity to cover her hands with his. 'The place is deserted. The hotel guests are on a trip to Land's End that Mawgan arranged and the staff are skiving as usual.'

'That's unfair!' blustered Mawgan.

Cavan gave a snort of exasperation, and Bethany dragged her hands away. 'No, it's not,' he said curtly. 'The hotel is as deserted as the *Mary Celeste* and there isn't even anyone on Reception. What kind of a business is that?' He fixed Mawgan with a hard, uncompromising stare. 'You gather that I've been inside,' he said through his teeth.

'Oh, hell!' groaned Mawgan, rolling his eyes up, and Bethany looked from one to the other, sensing trouble.

'That describes it adequately, I think,' agreed Cavan harshly. 'I repeat: has Bethany any idea of what you've done?'

Mawgan flushed and looked uncomfortable. 'Well...I told her that I got a firm to do the re-fit last February before the summer season began——'

'While you pushed off on a painting holiday,' scowled Cavan. 'I don't know why I left the arrangements to you. I must have been seized by temporary madness.'

Mawgan flushed. 'It's a mistake I'm putting right. In fact, if you hadn't turned up today, you would never have known the re-fit was a disaster,' he muttered. 'That's why Beth's here—to see what she can do to improve things. After next week the hotel will be empty and we'll make the place look OK again. Dammit, Cavan, what do you care? You haven't come to see what I've been doing for almost a year.'

'There's been nothing to bring me here,' said Cavan quietly. He turned to the bewildered Bethany. 'If you want to, you can stay with me——'

Her chin lifted. 'Is that what this is about? Good grief, Cavan, before I took up your offer it would have to be wall-to-wall breeze blocks and cold steel carpets in there.'

'Close,' said Cavan laconically. 'Well, there's a pair of oyster satin sheets waiting for you if you need them. I had the impression that you were on edge. The villagers might be stand-offish for a while and I thought you might need a bolt-hole—as you did before when you ran off into the blue yonder. This time I'm offering to make room for you——'

'Oh, sharing,' she said with light sarcasm, 'the Cavan Trevelyan multi-storey harem. No, thanks.'

'Your tongue hasn't got any blunter,' frowned Cavan. 'I meant that my yacht is at your disposal. With or without me.'

'Your yacht?' Following the curt angling of his head, she turned to look at the glorious ketch on the shimmering blue sea. She cocked an eyebrow at Cavan. 'That's yours? I saw it sail in ... So who drove the flashy red Aston Martin?' she asked calmly. 'One of your ticket-touts?'

'Your hostility is showing,' murmured Cavan, sounding pleased. 'I drove the car.'

'And I sailed the boat,' husked a honey-warm voice from somewhere directly behind him.

Cavan stepped aside, mercifully releasing Bethany, who grew wide-eyed at the pocket-sized vision in front of her. Mawgan was equally pole-axed, judging by his village-yokel stare.

'I think you know Tania,' drawled Cavan. 'Tania Blake.'

Tania held out a tiny hand glinting with diamonds. 'Hello, Beth. Long time since we were in that ghastly school uniform, isn't it?'

'Tania?' Bethany could hardly believe the transformation. From a dumpy village girl, Tania had become a gorgeous woman. She was dressed in a casual jogging suit, but it was Italian and pure silk, in a rich green which matched her eyes and also the emeralds that sparkled ostentatiously in her ears amid a tumble of artful blonde waves. Someone was footing an expensive clothes bill, by the looks of it, mused Bethany. Tania had always said she'd land a millionaire. Her stomach muscles clenched in a sudden spasm. Cavan must be that man, she thought bleakly.

'My, my! What a thick skin you've got, Beth! I'm amazed you're here, after what the villagers said about you,' said Tania spitefully, smiling when Bethany blanched.

Cavan reached out with his big fist, opened his palm and gently pressed it against Tania's neat rose-bud mouth. Tania's lashes fluttered at him appealingly. 'Shut it,' he said amiably, with a slight tightness in his jaw.

'You don't have to worry about me,' insisted Bethany bravely, determined to protect herself. 'I don't care what anyone thinks any more. I have no feelings left about the matter. I'm here purely for Mawgan's sake, nothing else——'

'I'm sorry you don't care, Bethany,' said Cavan in a soft growl, removing his hand from Tania's mouth. 'I always did think you suppressed your feelings too much at the time of Dan's death instead of letting them fly.'

'Was that why you deliberately made me cry?' she asked huskily, remembering his cruelty.

'Oh, you remember that,' he said softly, his eyes darkening. 'You were like a zombie. I had to really work hard on you before you would burst into tears.'

'And you enjoyed every minute,' muttered Bethany in resentment.

'He did say at the time that you weren't acting normally,' put in Mawgan awkwardly. 'He said you needed something to jerk you out of your shock.'

'He did that all right,' she said flatly.

'I suppose,' husked Tania with deceptive sympathy, 'it didn't help having half a million pounds landing in your lap.'

Cavan's brooding eyes flickered briefly at Tania and then returned to the white-faced Bethany. Seagulls screamed and wheeled overhead, and she wanted to give vent to her own feelings by screaming too. The staggering sum of compensation paid out so quickly on Dan's accidental death on the oil rig had brought her nothing but misery.

'Still living off the money?' queried Cavan. His piercing stare bored a path of glittering ice into Bethany's soul, and she flinched noticeably. Her reaction made a contemptuous smile touch his lips. 'You are. Dammit, Bethany, you're wasting your talents,' he said, when she didn't deny his assumption that she was a lady of leisure.

'What I do is my business. I'm twenty-six, not twelve. You can't try to run my life for me any more.'

Bethany felt too unsettled by his intrusive questions to tell him the truth. In actual fact, she'd given away every penny of the compensation. Her whole outfit was three years old, but he wasn't to know that because its lines were classic and everlasting. She had no intention of letting him find out that she had been living hand to mouth, unable to find design work, standing behind the ticket counter of a local theme park all summer. She was Cornish, and proud.

'Beth's going to use her talents,' reminded Mawgan, 'on the hotel.'

'She'll need them,' remarked Cavan cynically. 'You've damn near ruined it.'

Bethany's mouth compressed when she saw Mawgan's hurt expression. 'I want to judge for myself,' she said curtly. 'Let me go. I'm not one of your bar-room girls, Cavan Trevelyan!'

'So you acknowledge my name at last,' he observed grimly, his big face filling her vision. 'I remember when a teacher called me Trevelyan you whirled on your lace-up brogues so fast that your socks fell down and your plaits stung your face, and you yelled out to all and sundry that I had not a drop of Trevelyan blood in my veins and had no right to use the name.'

Tania giggled merrily, and Bethany blushed with shame. What a welcome she'd given him! She'd been wrong. But then, she'd been only twelve, and horrified that her father should have married the big, hearty Rosie, who had filled the house with loud laughter. Bethany had been jealous that her position had been usurped in her father's heart and because Rosie had cheerfully taken over running the house. But Bethany had also taken her cue from the disapproving women of the village.

Rosie had been a barmaid from Plymouth, older than her father and with an illegitimate son—and such a son! There were wildfire rumours about him. No one had ever liked the fierce, surly sixteen-year-old Cavan who had stood up to every taunt and bullying attack and had given back better than he'd got. But Rosie's warm and jolly personality had soon melted opposition and had packed the bar at the Inn to overflowing.

'It was only natural that I was disturbed and upset,' defended Bethany.

Cavan nodded. 'That goes for me too. Coming here was a culture shock for me, after city life, city sophistication. Still, like you, I got out fast. You always said I needed a bigger stage where I could strut. Big, brash, common and showy, that's me, isn't it?' he mocked.

She looked at him doubtfully. Somehow he didn't fit that description she'd flung at him during one of their endless quarrels. He was more groomed, more quietly sure of himself, and she felt he was even controlling one or two emotions—though she was certain that the wild and violent spark still lay simmering inside. Tough guys didn't change their penchant for fisticuffs and confrontation overnight.

'You said it,' she smiled coolly. 'Excuse me.' She turned towards the hotel and realised the old stone mullion windows had been double-glazed. She frowned.

'So you're going in?' asked Cavan quietly, noticing her hesitation. 'Tania, go and check on the Longchamp situation.'

'But——' pouted Tania.

'*Now*!' he barked.

Tania jumped and slid sulkily into Cavan's car, picking up a handset.

'She's well trained,' observed Bethany with distaste.

'Best secretary I ever had,' said Cavan with a bland smile.

The penny dropped. Bethany remembered that Tania had excelled at business studies. Judging by Cavan's enigmatic expression and Tania's air of possession, she also excelled in pleasing her boss in other ways. An uncharacteristic jealousy knifed through her with a startling thoroughness. Annoyed, she marched past Cavan and into the Inn. Two steps inside what had once been a slate-flagged hall, she stopped dead.

'You see what I mean,' panted Mawgan, coming up behind her and sounding as if he'd run with her case from the car. 'The décor isn't really suitable——'

'Not suitable——!' Words failed her.

'Come and have a drink.' Cavan's body pressed against hers and virtually forced her to move in the direction of the empty bar. The partition wall seemed to have disappeared. Numbly she let herself be propelled forwards, too dismayed to protest. 'Mawgan, get her a Cinzano, quick. I'll have a brandy.'

'At this hour? Lord! It's three o'clock——!' began Mawgan.

'Do it!' snapped Cavan sharply. Like Tania, Mawgan jumped to obey him. 'Can't you see your sister's overwhelmed at the extent of the alterations?' he growled.

'I hadn't realised they'd made such huge changes,' said Bethany slowly. 'It's not my home any longer.'

The cosy, intimate atmosphere of the old beamed lobby, bar and restaurant had disappeared. Instead, a huge open space had been created, which glittered with chrome and glass. It would have been fine for a London wine-bar, but was totally inappropriate for Portallen. The character had been utterly lost. Her eyes widened at the uniformly dull modern prints on the walls.

'Mawgan!' she said in dismay. 'Where are your lovely paintings?'

'They didn't look right.' Mawgan sullenly poured himself a glass of cider. He came over and slid into the scarlet banquette beside Cavan. 'Look, I was tricked. I somehow signed a form giving them a free hand, and they unloaded some fittings that no one wanted. It was a mistake, and I'm putting it right.'

'Damn right you are,' growled Cavan. 'And it had better be at no cost to me. No wonder the takings are down. Not much call for yuppy pubs in Cornwall.'

'What else is different?' asked Bethany gently, seeing Mawgan was being put on the spot. 'The garden? The bedrooms?'

'You *are* out of touch, Bethany, aren't you?' muttered Cavan, glaring at Mawgan accusingly. 'And so was I. I should have come down here before, but... Tell us about the bedrooms, Mawgan,' he said grimly.

Her brother shifted in his seat. 'The bedrooms have been modernised in the same way, I'm afraid. Chrome and glass.'

'The four-poster beds?' asked Bethany anxiously.

'Stored in the attic. I was going to get them down, but then I didn't know what to do about the colour scheme. The brocade hangings didn't match the new check carpets,' he said helplessly. 'But the garden's un-changed, if a bit run down. I haven't had time——'

'The garden is a total shambles,' interrupted Cavan contemptuously. 'Like everything you do here. *Hell*, Mawgan! I'd throw you out of the damn window if it wasn't double-glazed and impossible to open!'

Mawgan leapt to his feet. 'It's your fault! You said I had to smarten the place up and I had to do it on the cheap. You kept issuing directives about making more profit and constantly criticising the way things were going! You *bombarded* me with memos and complaints. People don't have money to burn any more! You know that in the current economic——'

'Oh, don't excuse your inefficiency by blaming the lack of spending power on the populace in general,' snapped Cavan. 'You're a hopeless manager, that's the fact of the matter. Your staff pilfer from the till, and you sign the overtime chits without even checking them. Your stock-taking is non-existent and I imagine half of Portallen has smuggled drink out and is boozing away at home at my expense.'

'Don't you dare to insult my brother!' seethed Bethany. 'He's admitted to a mistake anyone could make. He couldn't do anything about it till the guests had departed, and he's done his best with little help from you, it appears, if you didn't even know what was going on in your own hotel.'

'Hotel?' Cavan's lip curled. 'I've had more complaints about the running of this so-called hotel than I've had from any of my East End pubs. Tell me, what do the locals think of the way you've changed their pub? What do the fishermen do, now you've removed the small Stable Bar?'

'A few still come in,' Mawgan said awkwardly.

'My mother would turn in her grave! Dammit, man, apart from being a local service and a meeting place, this pub survives in the winter by its local trade. Lose that, and...' Cavan shook his head in exasperation. 'You should have consulted me. It's my damn building!'

'Apparently you've never shown interest before,' Bethany pointed out stiffly.

'Well, all that is going to change,' Cavan said, giving her a challenging stare. 'I'm going to be around a lot more now.'

Her hand flew to her mouth, and she saw his predator's eyes go there, and the slow, sultry parting of his sensual lips. A quiver ran through her, as sharp and deep as if she'd been harpooned. Cavan's sexuality seared across the table at her, rendering her mute.

'I...I think I've got a few things to do,' said Mawgan, eyeing them both. 'Excuse me.'

Bethany thought there was the shadow of a smile on Cavan's lips, and she wanted to leave too, but her legs were leaden. She'd come here specifically to help Mawgan, knowing it would be an awkward situation because of the malicious stories which had been spread about her in the past. She'd even steeled herself to the probability that she'd see Cavan once or twice. But she hadn't bargained on this.

'You don't need to stay in Portallen,' she said huskily, longing to moisten her dry mouth but knowing he'd find that infinitely provocative. All his girlfriends had declared in awe that he was incredibly over-sexed. 'I am perfectly capable of restoring the character of the hotel at the minimum cost to you.'

He didn't reply at first, but studied her minutely, inch by inch, and she had to force herself to act normally under the disconcerting pressure of his gaze. Then he nodded. 'I know that.'

His eyes had reached her shapely breasts, firm against the fabric of her jacket. Without seeing any need to hurry, he let his gaze slide over her waist and—aided and abetted by the glass-topped table—to her slender stockinged thighs, visible beneath the fashionably short skirt.

'Looking for signs of my alleged dissolute life?' she asked haughtily, trying to divert his attention from her legs.

'Surprisingly, the effects are not showing yet. In fact, you look as if you've spent the last two years sitting in a beauty parlour,' commented Cavan sardonically.

She made her eyes crawl contemptuously up the kind of chest that any navvy would display with pride. 'And you look as if you've been heaving bricks and building one,' she retorted defensively.

He laughed shortly and leaned forwards, his strongly featured face a little too close to hers for comfort. 'Life good for you, is it? Money in the bank, no reason to work, men fawning all over you?' he murmured.

His hand lifted, and she waited with tense anticipation as his forefinger slowly uncurled and lightly stroked her cheek. Some of her blusher came off on to his finger and he smiled into her eyes. Bethany trembled involuntarily. And saw his eyes narrowing.

'Life is a ball,' she lied, thinking how deceptive appearances could be and floundering for some form of normal conversation. 'How's the underworld these days?'

'Ticking along,' he said nonchalantly. 'Like Captain Hook's crocodile in *Peter Pan*. Remember the crocodile who swallowed a clock? It ticked so loudly that everyone could run to safety. That's me. I give everyone a chance to escape a savaging from me. Just one chance,' he added with soft menace.

'I suppose you're expecting me to ask what happens when people have had that one chance,' she said, trying to sound indifferent to his answer even though her nerves were on edge.

'Clever girl,' he said approvingly with devastating patronage. 'Obviously I eat them for breakfast.'

Bethany met his relentless gaze boldly, only just managing to remain composed. 'I must remember to remove my earrings so you don't get too much roughage, then,' she said drily.

Cavan gave her one of his dazzling smiles. She picked up her Cinzano, using the gesture as an excuse to drop her lashes and avoid his eyes. He was as hard as nails and as ruthless as any pirate on the high seas, and he had some nasty treat in store for her, she was certain. There was a definite air of smugness about the set of his mouth.

'I've missed you, Bethany,' said Cavan quietly.

Totally disarmed by the unexpectedness of his remark, she hurriedly placed her drink on the table before he had a chance to notice the way she was shaking. To her alarm, her hand was covered by his. Her big Celtic-blue eyes lifted. He seemed serious. What was he trying to do to her?

She waited for the punchline, the joke, the ridicule. A long, tense silence stretched between them and she found herself incapable of breaking it or of avoiding the extraordinary pull of his unnervingly softened blue eyes—soft as the silken water in Portallen Harbour, as deep, as treacherous, she thought wildly.

Her fingers were gripped tightly and raised to his lips, and he never stopped looking at her while he did this, not even when he curled her hand over and kissed the palm, sending tiny shivers through her body. She still ached for him, then. The knowledge filled her with misery. He had a terrible and inexplicable hold over her. If he should ever become aware of it, he'd do just what he'd said—eat her for breakfast.

'Bethany, there's something I must say to you,' husked Cavan, his breath on her face making her shiver.

'Darling! Sorry to butt in, but Johnny's on the phone from the Dorchester.' Tania was bending close to Cavan, her hand possessively on his broad shoulder, her blonde curls softly sweeping his jaw. A waft of expensive perfume drifted over to Bethany.

Cavan's mouth quirked and he gently placed Bethany's hand back on the table. 'Your timing is appalling, Tania,' he drawled, still holding Bethany's eyes. 'You may be a good secretary and an even better sailor, but you have no appreciation of a tense and highly charged atmosphere.'

'Oh, you're wrong, I do,' demurred Tania. 'That's why I phoned Johnny in the first place and why I interrupted.'

'You——!' Cavan chuckled at Tania's pert smile. 'My saviour,' he said fondly to her, giving her bottom a very familiar and insolently chauvinistic slap. She wriggled and giggled, her eyes flirting with his. 'Excuse me, Bethany. We'll talk later about your brother's job—and how I see your role.'

Her eyes widened. 'Is that what you were going to say just now?' she blurted out.

'Of course. What were you expecting?' he murmured, rising from the seat, mocking her with his dark, steady gaze.

'Almost anything, knowing you... Wait a minute! His job? My role? What do you mean——?' Bethany half rose in agitation, but he gave her a mysterious smile and she was left facing the triumphant Tania.

'He'll explain,' said Tania in an offhand manner. 'He has plans for you.'

'Plans? Oh, no. I won't let that man manipulate me,' declared Bethany with determination. 'I have my own plans, and he doesn't come anywhere in them.'

'Is that so? I thought for a minute you were contemplating a merger,' said Tania coldly.

'With Cavan? You can't have forgotten,' frowned Bethany, 'that we've been at daggers drawn since he stormed into my life at the age of sixteen and proceeded to turn this house upside-down! It was like having a flame-thrower in the house! No, thanks. I'd rather merge with a ticking crocodile.'

Tania frowned, not having had the benefit of Cavan's earlier remark. 'His arrival certainly sparked us all,' she agreed. 'It was dull before he came. He's so *passionate*. Portallen came alive, didn't it?' she sighed wistfully.

'Yes, I suppose it did,' Bethany said with reluctance. Cavan had been rough and ready, spoiling for a fight, but had brought with him a breath of fresh air and vitality which had made the sleepy village fizz. For a moment, Bethany saw the old Tania; teased by the boys because she was overweight and mooning hopelessly over the dynamic, exciting and hot-headed Cavan. 'We were friends, then, you and I,' she said quietly.

'You dumped me when the boys started hanging around you,' Tania remarked with a sullen expression.

'Oh, Tania!' Bethany said, hurt. 'That's not true! You left me with them——'

'Because I was in the way,' snapped Tania. 'The boys made that clear enough with their hurtful comments. But now I'm equipped to get what I want, and, in case you haven't realised, what I want is Cavan. Leave him alone, Beth. Stop flashing those endless legs of yours at him and giving him those long, sultry looks.' Her small face grew sharp and a little desperate. 'I've worked hard to hook him and I don't want some flash millionairess distracting him by waving wads of bank notes around. He's not for sale or even for hire.'

'Is that what you think? You don't know Cavan very well,' retorted Bethany, feeling a brief, unreasoning dislike for her old schoolfriend. She ought to feel sorry for her, because Tania apparently imagined she could 'land' the slippery East End charmer. 'Cavan has always been available to the highest bidder. Money is his only God, his only love. It sends him into ecstasies. He left here to make his fortune, and he's achieved that ambition. He'd sell his mother if she was on the market— and take a discount for cash.'

Disconcerted by the extraordinary bitterness of her words, she swept out to the kitchen in search of Mawgan, leaving Tania gripping the side of the banquette in suppressed rage.

Bethany paused in the corridor, gathering her composure. It was becoming a little frayed at the ends. Once again, she was in danger of being destroyed by Cavan. She closed her eyes briefly, vowing to herself that he wouldn't succeed.

The situation might seem like a normal clash between a stepbrother and his stepsister on the surface, but she knew better. The scurrilous poison-pen letters had almost wrecked her confidence and had driven her from the home and the brother she loved. And it had been Cavan who had written them.

CHAPTER TWO

BETHANY clenched her fists. Yes, Cavan had begun the smear campaign. Who else had actively disliked her and had known so much about her? The truth had been twisted quite expertly, by someone who had hated and resented her, making it easy for the recipients of the letters to believe the dreadful stories.

Slowly the rumours had spread: she'd left Portallen as a teenager because she was pregnant; she'd married Dan purely for his money; in Aberdeen she'd 'entertained' oil-riggers on leave while Dan was on shift duty. The letters had accused her of being a merry widow and sleeping with half the males in Portallen because she had an insatiable sexual appetite. If her light was on all night, there were knowing looks in the morning when she appeared, drained, exhausted. If she spoke to a male hotel guest, she was making an assignation. If she went for a walk, women followed her in case she was meeting their husbands or boyfriends. Men freely made lewd propositions to her.

Sometimes she had wanted to take a midnight stroll to think about her future without Dan. She'd been unable to, fearful of whom she might meet, or what the gossip would be the next day. So she became a prisoner in her own house, despised by people she'd thought of as friends. And Cavan had been responsible.

The sheer vindictiveness had been hard to take. Her doctor had explained that rumour-mongering wasn't unusual when an inhabitant of a tightly knit community suddenly became wealthy. He said she'd stepped out of their world and returned a stranger, that their hostility was bound up in the fact that she'd rejected them by leaving. He'd recommended a new start somewhere far away.

For a long while now she'd been convinced that it had been Cavan who manipulated the stories, who had turned the village against her. They'd squabbled from the very first. He'd disliked her so much that he'd avoided her as much as possible. Their rows had become a standing joke. Yet it was from the time she'd announced her intention to marry Dan that he'd become unbearable, as if he had resented her for marrying into money instead of working for it like him.

Bethany tipped her head back and wondered what Cavan had in store for her this time. And suddenly she felt a fierce, stubborn determination that he wouldn't succeed in driving her from her childhood home until she was good and ready to go under her own terms. She'd survive. She always had. It would be a matter of existing, not living, but then she'd forgotten what it was like to be really happy.

At least she was with Mawgan, at least she was in Portallen. A little more optimistic, she pushed open the door to the kitchen. She smiled. Mawgan *had* made an excuse to leave her with Cavan; he didn't have any jobs to do at all—he was sitting hunched over a cup of tea and a plate of pasties.

'Hi, Beth. Are you mad at me for ruining our home?'

Smiling, she shook her head, letting her anger with Cavan and Tania evaporate, and automatically went over to the hob to light the gas beneath the kettle. Mercifully the kitchen was the same: the old wood-burning Aga, low beams, huge stone butler's sink and the enormous pine table in the middle of the room. She sat down, suddenly tired.

'You'd better put me properly in the picture,' she said quietly. 'I need to know what money I have to play around with.'

'Not much,' answered Mawgan ruefully. 'I haven't saved a lot from the salary Cavan pays me. Canvases and oils are so expensive nowadays. Have you any cash to spare?'

'Not a penny,' sighed Bethany. She'd bought a cottage on Bodmin from the proceeds of the sale of her effects in Aberdeen, and there had been little left to live on. 'All the compensation went towards the Inshore Lifeboat. No one knows about that, do they?' she asked anxiously.

'No. Why didn't you let me tell them? It might have altered their opinion of you.' Mawgan bit into his pasty and chewed for a moment. 'They never dreamed the donation came from you. They thought it was Cavan.'

'Him? He wouldn't give his hard-fought money away,' she said tartly. 'No one must know it was my compensation money. The villagers would be mortified. *You* wouldn't accept any of it, and you're my brother.'

'It was good of you, Beth, but I couldn't go through art college on a dead man's money,' said Mawgan quietly.

'I know what you mean. I never liked the idea of being given cash in exchange for Dan's life,' she admitted. 'But . . . I wish you'd approached me sooner for help. I could have done the re-fit myself in February, at cost-price.'

'Six months ago you weren't ready to come back,' Mawgan pointed out. 'I had only to mention Portallen and you went as white as chalk and dropped things. I'll have to borrow the money somehow, though God knows where from.'

'Cavan?' she suggested reluctantly. 'It's his hotel. He might cough up, now that he's seen it needs doing.'

Mawgan looked up hopefully. 'He didn't sound too keen earlier. But a loan... Would you ask him? He'd do it for you.'

'You're joking! Only if he thought he'd get something in return,' she said ruefully. Mawgan seemed upset, and she touched his hand in concern. 'What's the matter? There's something else worrying you, isn't there?'

He grunted. 'I think Cavan's come down here to throw me out.'

'What? Sack you? But it's your home! We were brought up here!' she cried in horror. 'He can't do that to you. Five generations of Trevelyans have lived in this building! Oh, Mawgan, he'll sell it to some property developer for a fat profit! That man has got no soul, no decency, no sense of honour!' she seethed. 'He's like a basking shark, cruising around for someone to savage!'

Mawgan shifted awkwardly in his seat. 'He's not that bad. I did make a mess of things. My mind was on painting. I've been working on a series of canvases... I can't excuse my vagueness. He's going to give me an ultimatum, I know.'

'Damn right I am!' They both whirled at Cavan's tight, clipped voice. 'No soul, no decency, no sense of honour, eh?' Bethany flushed, but defied him with a look. Her brother was in trouble, and Cavan was causing it. 'The basking *shark*,' continued Cavan angrily, 'is currently gnashing his teeth and looking for some rotten piece of carrion to tear into bite-sized chunks—and I think I've found my pound of flesh,' he bit, looking directly at her.

'How dare you?' she said, her voice low with rage. 'If anything's rotten around here, it's you.'

'You know nothing about me. Not how I work, what I've done, what I do now,' he rasped. 'You make assumptions all the time. You're blind to what's in front of your nose, Bethany Trevelyan, and I'm going to open

your eyes good and wide.' He reached down and hauled
her to her feet, giving her a sharp shake, and when
Mawgan moved forwards in outraged protest he turned
his back on him, effectively preventing Mawgan from
coming to her rescue. 'You bitch,' he muttered, for her
ears only. 'Wait till I've finished with you. You'll wish
you'd never fluttered those two-coat-mascara eyelashes
at me.'

'Cavan!' cried Mawgan urgently. 'This wasn't what
we——'

'Shut up!' ordered Cavan as Mawgan tried vainly to
shoulder his way in.

'Let me go,' Bethany gasped. 'I don't know what
you're talking about. And if you think you can threaten
me and interfere in my life——'

'Why not? You interfered in mine,' said Cavan curtly,
suddenly letting her drop unceremoniously to the chair.

She rubbed her faintly bruised bottom resentfully,
glaring at him from under her brows. 'Me?' she asked
in amazement.

'Every minute of every day,' he breathed, his chest
rising up and down rapidly. Bethany looked at him in
alarm. For some reason he was building up into one of
his spectacular rages. 'From the moment I stepped into
this house with my mother, you tried to make my life
hell, you selfish, unwelcoming little——'

'That's enough!' rapped Mawgan. 'You're going too
far. You always did. Admit it; you did throw your weight
about a bit at first. Bethany was only trying to stop you
bossing us around.'

'No,' he denied quietly, his eyes riveted on the white-
lipped Bethany. 'She has always wanted to be the centre
of attention. She resented my mother and resented me.
Selfish little girl! Well, she got what she wanted, didn't
she? With a vengeance. She became the centre of at-

tention all right.' He tipped up Bethany's chin with a rough, hurting finger and thumb which bit into her soft flesh. 'And you didn't like it, did you? The gawping Press, the gossip, the foul accusations, the resentment——'

'Oh, you bastard,' she whispered shakily. 'You evil, cruel, heartless bastard!'

His eyes closed momentarily as if in pain. 'That's me,' he said bitterly. 'And you made me one, pushing my patience to its limit as you did just now. You, a twelve-year-old girl, had the power to hit all my raw nerves bang on target by telling me I didn't belong and never would, constantly pointing out my ignorance of country ways, lighting my short fuse. You, at eighteen, teased and tormented all the young men in the village till their tongues were hanging out——'

'That's not true!' she gasped.

'You never dated any of them, and they asked often enough,' Cavan went on relentlessly. 'You pranced around in skin-tight T-shirts and brief shorts and that incredible scrap of a blue bikini——'

'What? They were hand-me-downs from the jumble sale,' she cried indignantly, flushing at the scornful curl of his lip. 'I deny that I knew I was being provocative——'

'Oh, come off it, Bethany!' sneered Cavan. 'I *told* you to cover up. I warned you that you couldn't go clambering about on the rocks and sunbathing on the beach half-naked without raising the blood-pressure of every male in sight. You knew well enough.'

Her lashes swept down to cover her guilty eyes. Yes. When he'd told her that, she'd become intensely aware of the potency of her body. Desperately infatuated with the handsome Cavan, she had deliberately wandered about in what she'd hoped were alluring and womanly clothes, hoping he would fall for her and stop tormenting her by flirting with every other female in the village. Instead, he'd become even more bad-tempered than before.

'I didn't tease the boys,' she insisted. 'I didn't mean to, anyway,' she amended.

'You were a lot of things from the age of sixteen to eighteen, Bethany, but you weren't innocent,' scorned Cavan. 'Oh, you knew what you were doing, all right, practising your come-hither glances on the boys—and on me, whenever I appeared. And then, dammit, as soon as you'd perfected them, you jumped into the lap of the first man with money who had the misfortune to stay here and be dazzled by your seductive body. If I'm a bastard, it's because of you and the cynical impression I formed of women from your calculating, cold-blooded example.'

'That's ridiculous——' she cried.

'And when you came back to the village after Dan died it was the same,' he continued unsparingly. 'The men flocked around you like seagulls behind a plough. You arrived with a tarnished reputation and certainly left with one.' His hand slid down to her throat, hovering there, and to her alarm she saw a murderous glint in his cold eyes. 'But now I've had experience of many, many women, and know exactly how to deal with you,' he said in a tone of soft menace.

His threat hung in the air. Bethany stared into his merciless and malevolent eyes, and felt the crackling hostility which leapt backwards and forwards between them. She let out a harsh, croaking sound of protest.

'Cavan, I think you'd better get out of here,' grated Mawgan, his voice quivering with anger. 'And let go of Bethany before I offer you a knuckle sandwich with the compliments of the management.'

'I will leave when I want to and not before. I *own* Portallen,' snapped Cavan, nevertheless releasing his hold on Bethany. Her eyes blazed and kindled an answering fire in his. 'You hate that, don't you?' he said, taunting her. 'You loathe the fact that mother inherited the hotel when your father died, and that after her death it came to me.'

'Of course I hate it,' she said proudly. 'Because you don't deserve it, because you don't feel the same way about it. It's Mawgan's by rights. You were only our stepbrother and you had no time for the hotel, the village or the villagers. Your heart was always in the city, with the bright lights and gaudy women.'

Cavan smiled coldly. 'My heart? What heart?' he mocked. Bethany set her chin stubbornly, and he gave it an insolent tweak then turned to Mawgan. 'OK. Enough of this. Sit down, Mawgan. I've got something to tell the pair of you.'

'Oh, lord!' groaned Mawgan. 'I know what's coming. You're going to give me the sack.'

'Got it in one,' said Cavan bluntly.

'Cavan, you can't. You have a moral obligation to let us both live here if we want to,' asserted Bethany in desperation, seeing how pale Mawgan looked. She wouldn't let Cavan hurt her brother. She'd stuck up for Mawgan all her life, and would defend her family home with the same ferocity if necessary.

Cavan gave a derisive laugh. 'Moral? Me?' He shook his head emphatically. 'Morality doesn't enter into it. I've come to a decision and I never change my mind. I'm offering you both a choice. One chance each, Bethany.'

'A chance? Then he can stay on as manager?' she asked hopefully.

Turning to her brother, Cavan smiled with deceptive innocence. 'You think a lot of this place, don't you, Mawgan? How keen are you to keep it in the Trevelyan family?'

'Don't answer that!' shot Bethany. 'He'll use whatever you say to some crooked purpose.'

Cavan ignored her. 'Mawgan, you make a rotten manager. I kept you on because of your ties here. Out of the goodness of my heart.' He ignored, too, Bethany's snort of disbelief. 'This might be paradise to you, but to me it's a business on a profit-and-loss sheet. I can't let this place go to rack and ruin, and I can't stand inefficiency of any kind.'

'I've tried——' began Mawgan.

'That's not good enough. I want achievers, not triers. It's a matter of authority,' interrupted Cavan brutally. 'And you haven't got it. I want you out.' He paused, his hard eyes boring into Mawgan's. 'You have a week's notice,' he said curtly.

'A week? You can't do that!' cried Bethany, springing immediately to her startled brother's defence.

'How would you stop me?' murmured Cavan, turning smoky blue eyes on her. 'Bargain with the devil?'

She paused, her instincts telling her to back away. He wanted something from her, she was convinced of that. Yet Mawgan's livelihood was on the line.

'If need be,' she said coldly, her hands trembling with apprehension.

'Good. Exactly what I was hoping,' he declared with barely suppressed triumph, and Bethany's heart sank. 'Mawgan, leave us. Your sister and I have something to discuss.'

'Like hell I will! With you in this mood? No way. Besides, you said I had a choice——'

'The choice depends on Bethany,' said Cavan smugly, as if he had just landed a prize fish.

'Cavan, when we talked, you said——' began Mawgan.

'I said, when we spoke on the telephone, that it was time your sister faced the realities of normal life, and that I knew how to force her to do so,' growled Cavan.

Bethany's eyes darted backwards and forwards to Mawgan and Cavan. 'Oh, Mawgan,' she groaned, 'what have you done?'

'It was all he said,' cried her brother in distress. 'He never told me he was coming here, or that it meant I'd get the sack or...'

He paused, and Bethany tried to interpret the look which passed between the two men. It was as if Cavan was signalling to Mawgan. 'What is going on?' she asked suspiciously.

'I'm warning him,' said Cavan implacably. 'The more he says, the harder it will be for us all.'

'For you to force me to face life?' she scorned. 'My God, Cavan! You've got a nerve!'

'You can't jet-set around forever,' said Cavan grimly.

Bethany and Mawgan stared at him, and she remembered that no one knew she was virtually broke and had been living like a recluse for the last two years—and for the whole summer, walking three miles to work, sitting alone in a small wooden hut all day and walking back again. So much for the glamorous life he imagined she was leading. The thought that the great Cavan Trevelyan had some misinformation cheered her up and gave her strength.

'It's OK, I can handle him,' she said to her brother. 'He's no problem—not compared with a whole village hurling abuse at me.'

However, when the disgruntled Mawgan reluctantly left, Bethany turned to the impatiently waiting Cavan with a leaden heart. He wanted to hurt her. If he did but know, he could do so easily with one callous, brutal kiss. Her knees buckled and she folded them under her as she collapsed with as much grace as she could into the deep armchair by the Aga.

'Oh, the legs approach,' mocked Cavan in derision. 'Who was it who said you had yards of them, up to your armpits?'

'You,' said Bethany with commendable calm.

He grinned. 'So I did. How well they'll look, draped over a big, cosy sofa. Any visiting guests will love them.' His head tipped on one side as he surveyed her from head to toe.

His smouldering gaze was worrying. A heavy sensuality filled the air, projected with such a compelling force that it made her body tingle. Bethany felt the panic building up inside her, spiralling tightly, urgent to escape. 'What are you talking about?' she asked with great indifference.

'You're a class act. You and your legs would fit in perfectly here—once it's been done up properly.' He half lowered his heavy eyelids, his eyes mesmeric beneath them.

Bethany swallowed and tried to keep her mind on what he was saying. 'I'm not having anything to do with any guests. If you think I'd make a good waitress or a receptionist, you're mistaken. Are you being funny?' she asked frostily.

'No.' He came over and crouched in front of her, intimidatingly close, a habit of his which she found irritating in the extreme. 'I want to put Mawgan through art college,' he said, watching carefully for her reaction. He wasn't disappointed.

Bethany's eyes had widened in amazement at the bombshell. 'You? Why?' she gasped.

'Because he's a square peg in a round hole here and because he's very talented. Raw, untaught, but talented. We've both grown up with his paintings. I know how well they compare with professional work.' His eyes mocked her stunned face.

'There must be a profit in it for you somewhere,' she said caustically.

'You're right,' he acknowledged. 'It would be an investment, you understand. I have every intention of taking a percentage of his future earnings. He'd be my protégé. You know, Bethany, I never understood why you didn't cough up some of your compensation for him, so that he could do what he's always wanted to do.'

'It's really none of your business, but we discussed it,' she said, her voice neutral. 'He refused the money. Partly pride, partly because he couldn't bear to see anyone else running Portallen. I did try to persuade him. He was adamant.'

'Well, as sure as hell he's not going to run the hotel any more, so he might as well go to college,' he said laconically. 'I could even find him markets in my pubs and some of the hotels I know. There are countless bare walls around, waiting for paintings as good as his.'

'And?' prompted Bethany cynically, knowing that wasn't all. Mawgan would agree. He'd sell his soul to be able to paint all day. Cavan would get his ten per cent and she... She gulped.

Cavan laughed softly, one big hand resting on her knee. 'For a woman with a limited education, you're very quick on the uptake,' he commented insultingly. 'You can read my mind like a book, can't you?'

'There aren't many pages and the words are simple,' she said tartly. He gave her a suspiciously innocent grin, and the hand crept upwards. 'Slide that any higher and I'll slap your face,' warned Bethany. 'No man touches me.' Cavan removed his hand as if it had touched fire. 'Get to the point,' she muttered.

'Even before I saw the bodged re-fit, I'd decided that it was time the Portallen Inn was revamped and pushed up-market for the luxury trade. You know the kind of thing I mean: choice of bath oils, quality fittings, subtle furnishings in keeping with the age of the place——'

'It's thirteenth century. Do you mean trestle-tables, roast boar's head and straw on the floor?' she asked flippantly, furious with herself for wishing that his hand had stayed on her thigh. Where it had been, the skin was cold.

She suddenly felt desolate and lonely. And painfully aware of the gnawing ache in her body. Cavan mixed up all her emotions. Too often she became shrewish, bitter and shallow—all because she wanted him and always had, adored him and always had, was bewildered and resentful about her uncontrollable need. You ought to be able to hate someone without tossing about every night wanting them too, she thought crossly.

Cavan evidently didn't find her remark amusing. He was scowling at her, his heavy brows drawn together, his lips tight and disapproving.

'Careful. The shark is a notoriously bad-tempered beast,' he reminded her grimly. 'I take a certain amount of backchat and then I retaliate. Don't push your luck, Bethany. There isn't time for clever remarks. I want this place ready to open for the Christmas trade.'

She laughed in his face. 'Good heavens! Even you will never get anyone to turn Portallen into an up-market country hotel in that time!'

'Oh, yes, I will,' he said quietly. 'You.'

Bethany looked at Cavan with growing horror as she realised he was deadly serious. 'Not me!' she breathed.

'The kettle's been boiling for some time,' he murmured. 'Shall we have tea?' Calmly, under her startled gaze, he filled the pot and placed two mugs on the table.

She stared at them numbly. 'I came here to help Mawgan,' she said slowly, her brain refusing to function.

'And so you shall,' soothed Cavan, sitting opposite her and spooning in an unseemly amount of sugar. 'My way.'

'No! If Mawgan's going to college, there's no reason for me to stay at all,' she said hastily, resisting his blatant manipulation of them both. 'I certainly don't want to do any work for you.'

'Oh, dear. No co-operation from you, no art college,' said Cavan blandly.

She stared at him helplessly. '*Why?*'

His eyes mocked her confusion. 'Before I answer, hear the prize you get for completing the renovations in time,' he told her in his resonant voice.

'Prize?' She frowned irritably.

'Yes. It's not a bad one. A bribe. You get Portallen.'

Bethany blinked. There must be a catch. He'd never hand it over just like that. 'I don't believe you! Why——?'

'Work for me, finish the contract, and the hotel will revert to your family,' he said quietly as if he meant every word.

Bethany's mind was whirling at the implications of the deal. It made sense in the kind of contorted logic Cavan used. After all, he was a confirmed bachelor, playing the field happily from all accounts. He'd have no family to leave his fortune to, and in any case he didn't care anything about Portallen, so he was perfectly prepared to dangle one insignificant hotel in front of her eyes as a bribe. Her mouth became grim. He was obsessed with getting his own way.

'That would mean that I'd have to stay here till Christmas,' she said doubtfully.

'Are you afraid?' he queried. 'Didn't you just say you cared nothing for the villagers and their sharp tongues?'

Hung by her own lies. They'd been brave lies, flung in Cavan's face, the words torn from her by her own pride and his ever-present threat to dominate and crush her. She shrugged helplessly.

'I can't stay that long,' she said in a low voice. 'I have my own cottage on Bodmin——' Her eyes flew up to his in dismay that she'd revealed what she and Mawgan had kept from everyone.

'*Bodmin*? You? Good God!' he marvelled in a lazy drawl. 'I'd never have believed it! I'd imagined you hitting the nightclubs and fashion shops somewhere in Paris or Rome, since you were nowhere to be found in London.'

Bethany tensed. 'Why do you say that? Did you try to find me?' she demanded.

'Oh, Bethany Lowena Trevelyan, I've been trawling the city streets looking for you for ages,' he said huskily, a mocking look in his eloquent eyes.

The distance between them seemed to shrink, and the room closed in around them, the low ceiling pressing in on her. It was as if she and Cavan swam in a warm golden glow, suspended in mid-air... Bethany gritted her teeth and cursed her wild imagination. It was only the sunshine pouring in through the lattice window and the warmth generated by the Aga. And her own crazy dreams.

'What for?' she asked flatly.

'To revamp the hotel, of course; what else could I have in mind?'

He was lying. That soft growl was purring with sexual innuendo. She was afraid he'd force her to do more than work for him. He'd use any kind of threat—perhaps say he was going to withdraw financial support from Mawgan if she wasn't nice to him. He wanted her submission. He'd made that plain long ago. She bit her lip.

'I wouldn't know,' she lied. 'Something nasty. I don't have much experience of men like you.'

He smiled as if that were a compliment. 'There aren't many of us around,' he sympathised. 'Anyway, I've had the idea for a long time. I knew Portallen was losing money, and that Mawgan hadn't the temperament to be a good manager.'

'There are hundreds of people who could do the renovations.'

'I know. I wanted you.'

She winced at the quick pain that shot through her ribs. Those were the very words she'd longed for him to say, all these years, from the moment she first set eyes on him and he'd thrown her burgeoning teenage emotions into disarray.

'Why?' she asked guardedly.

'God, Bethany, I wish you wouldn't pout like that. It's an open invitation, and makes men want to kiss you,' frowned Cavan. 'Come on, you know me. I want you to do it because I want to control you, and this will offer me the means.'

'C-c-control?' she spluttered, beside herself with fury.

'Of course. You see,' he said, ignoring her gasp of amazement at his nerve, 'you're the only person I've ever met whom I haven't been able to dominate. It's like...like never quite mastering one's backhand in tennis. Irritating. Something unfinished, you understand.'

'Tennis? If I had a racket in my hands you'd discover how good my backhand is,' she grated. 'You're power-mad! You'll never control me, never!'

He shrugged his broad shoulders as if conceding the point. 'Well, I thought I'd try. I must say,' he laughed, 'I never thought you lived in Cornwall still! I'd concentrated on searching Knightsbridge and the restaurants where celebrities hang out. Mawgan refused to give me your address. When I didn't find you, I imagined you'd fled abroad.'

'I don't want to leave Cornwall again. You seem to have gone to a lot of bother to get someone to decorate a hotel,' she observed.

'Not someone. You. I told you. I hadn't finished with you,' he smiled. 'So I had to find you some other way.'

She froze and then let her eyes flick up to his. Somehow she knew that her presence here wasn't the result of a decision between Mawgan and herself or even a casual telephone call between the two men. Cavan's expression was unreadable, but she'd seen a glint of amusement and self-satisfaction sweep across his face when she'd looked up and caught him watching her.

She licked her lips and bridled at Cavan's speculative glance. He was earthier, hungrier and more dangerous than she remembered, his whole body charged with sexual tension. His lips softened to a sultry line beneath her panic-stricken gaze and a wash of warm sensuality filled her with a weakening languor.

Bethany fought up to the surface, refusing to let his carnal desire swamp her senses. And then she realised what he'd done. 'You are the most unscrupulous, vile and unprincipled man I've ever met,' she said in a hard tone, her eyes a dark granite. 'You deliberately put the screws on Mawgan, didn't you, pressuring him, knowing he'd buckle?'

'Yes,' he confirmed easily.

'Oh!' she gasped. 'You don't even mind admitting it! Don't you care about his feelings? I wouldn't put it past you to have personally arranged for that crooked firm to make a mess of doing up the hotel.'

'I hadn't thought of that,' said Cavan in admiration.

'I can't believe that you have the gall to admit forcing Mawgan into a corner,' she muttered. 'What do you think it's done for his self-esteem?'

'How else was I to lay my hands on you?' he asked mildly. 'It won't have done him any lasting damage, and it's only brought things to a head. He knows perfectly well he's not cut out to be a manager, and you know that too. I would have sacked him anyway and booted him in the direction of art college. I knew that eventually Mawgan would have to lean on you, as he's always done ever since he was a kid, and that I'd finally flush you from cover.'

'You swine! You made my brother half demented with worry just so that you could put me in a position of subservience to you. You are really quite beneath contempt!' she seethed.

'No. Practical,' he corrected. 'Don't forget that I was born in the East End and then spent half my formative years in a pub in Plymouth while my mother earned enough to keep us both. Life rather leaps up at you in places like that and grabs you by the throat. It's sink or swim. The sharks or you. You grow up fast. I became a shark myself. If I want something, I go for it—none of your genteel shilly-shallying around.' He eyed her speculatively. 'Well?'

'You honestly are serious? You want me to do a complete turnkey job between now and Christmas?' she asked numbly, still shell-shocked.

'A what?'

Bethany heaved a sigh. 'Turnkey. It means the decorator is responsible for every single item in the renovation of a property, even down to the books in the bookcase, the wine in the fridge and the tea in the tea-caddy.'

'How does it work?' asked Cavan, his eyes narrowed with interest.

She shrugged. 'The client leaves a large cheque and the house key and comes back several months later with an even larger cheque in settlement. They turn the key in the lock, walk in and begin living without even having to shop for groceries, a sewing kit or a teddy-bear.'

He grinned. 'I'll buy that. Yes. A turnkey; that will suit me fine. Though there are some things I want a say in which I'd prefer not to leave to you. Like the wine we'll stock.' He beamed at her appalled face. 'We'll have fun thrashing out what you'll do and what I'll do.'

'*We*? You and me together? Oh, no, that's not on, Cavan!' Quickly she realised she was betraying her fear of him, and sought an excuse. 'I'd be no good, you see. Better you should find someone else. I've lost most of my contacts——'

'Find them. Or the deal about Mawgan is off,' he said ruthlessly.

She closed her eyes. 'You're not being reasonable——'

'Me, reasonable? When was I ever?' he asked cynically. 'You must agree, I'm consistent. It can be done, Bethany, if you have the will and the incentive. You could start soon. I can find you the craftsmen when you want them. They'll work like hell for me because I'll put them on good piece rates. You only have to provide the ideas and the stylish eye, they'll interpret whatever you want.'

'It's impossible!' frowned Bethany.

Cavan heaved a deep sigh. 'Then I must sell to the highest bidder, and you lose Portallen through your own selfish fault.'

'That's blatant blackmail!' she complained. 'Look, you must see that I can't do it. I won't——'

'I fail to see why. Wouldn't you like to see Portallen looking beautiful and thriving again?' murmured Cavan seductively. 'Money no object? The garden restored, herbs and fresh vegetables for the kitchen, the herbaceous borders restocked, a few palm trees, a swimming-pool maybe? Antiques in every room, well-burnished brass on the walls——?'

'Don't,' she said miserably. He had her beaten, and he knew it. He was going to gloat next.

But he took her gently by the shoulders and made her look at him. 'I don't like to see Portallen run-down any more than you do,' he said quietly. 'Neither does Mawgan. Nor would your father, if he was alive. Do this turnkey job and make Portallen a place to be proud of. You might even enjoy it. Mawgan will be in his element in art college, and you'll be able to return to this cottage of yours on Bodmin at Christmas. Why Bodmin, for God's sake?' he asked with a frown.

'That's my business,' she said stiffly, trying to resist the temptation to put her head against his oddly comforting shoulder and howl.

'There can't be much call for interior designers out on the moors, or for gorgeous clothes like those,' he mused. 'So you must have been quite isolated and...' He went quiet. Bethany waited miserably for him to get tired of waiting for her response. 'Did you want to run away from it all?' he asked in a voice so full of compassion that Bethany had to screw up all her muscles against his tender, lulling tones. 'I hadn't honestly realised until this moment that the whole thing had affected you so badly.'

His hand began to stroke the nape of her neck, and she stiffened. 'I tried not to show that I was upset,' she muttered.

'You succeeded. We thought you were as hard as nails. You were hurt, then.'

His eyes had become sympathetic and the languorous touch of his fingers was unbearable. She'd reveal how pleasurable his caress was in a moment if he didn't stop. Desperately Bethany thought of a way out.

'Yes,' she said throatily, 'I was hurt. Mainly because of Dan. Because of his death.'

He released her immediately, as she'd known he would, his pride stung that she'd married Dan when she should have been gasping at his feet like the rest of the women in Cornwall, whether he wanted them or not.

He moved to look out of the window at the incoming tide, an angry-looking back to her. 'Look at the advantages,' he said curtly, returning to his persuasion. 'If I sack Mawgan and offer him this chance, he'll be forced to take the plunge into the art world and stop dithering on the edge. He'd be launched on a glittering career. You'd be doing a job you enjoy then returning to a life of leisured luxury and——'

'You said Portallen would revert to us,' she reminded him quickly, 'but you carefully omitted to say *when*. Another thing: do I get paid for my services?'

'Board and lodging. Nothing more. You're worth a cool half-million. You don't need money.' A smile crept to the corners of his mouth. 'You can get me, too, if you play your cards right.'

A small twinge of alarm prickled her nerves. 'That's it?' she asked coldly. 'The right to sleep and eat in what ought to be my own home and the offer of a night or two with a voracious shark?'

'Finish by Christmas to my satisfaction and you get a half-share in Portallen,' he said abruptly over his shoulder. 'That's what I meant about it reverting to a Trevelyan. I should have said *half* reverting.'

Bethany lifted her head slowly, terribly disappointed. 'Not all of it,' she said dully.

'Be thankful for small mercies. You'd have to do a bit more than flash a roll of wallpaper around to win all of it,' he grinned.

'Then I'll have to make do with half,' she retorted. 'I'll have that in writing, too.'

'Done.'

'My God! You mean that!' Her mind raced and her heart began to thud with excitement. Mawgan could have that half-share and he could have a home here forever if he wanted. And when he married, then his children would inherit. Portallen would belong to the Trevelyans again. A smile spread over her face.

'In case you're wondering,' murmured Cavan, 'I'm making this once-only offer of a half-share because I think it's the only way to get you to move that idle backside of yours and do the job properly.'

'No one's ever complained about my work before,' she challenged.

'No. I've heard. Where you learned to do it, I don't know. You brought home some good artwork from school, but you weren't as talented as Mawgan. Did Dan pay for you to attend a course or something?' he asked curiously.

'Or something,' she agreed, her eyes wistful as she remembered. Cavan shifted impatiently, and she started guiltily.

'I want to know,' he said curtly. 'If I'm employing you I have a right to know your qualifications. So tell me.'

'I'm not qualified. But I have a good deal of experience.'

'How?'

'Accident, really. Dan was out on the oil rigs for weeks on end, and I got a bit bored,' she explained. 'I'd done up our home in Aberdeen and had helped a few friends with their decorating schemes. I found I had an instinctive flair for it. When Dan was sent to the Mexican Gulf, I took up interior decorating in a big way, preparing homes for whoever was flown out there by the company.'

'Pity you gave it up,' commented Cavan. 'Do you honestly *like* doing nothing all day other than counting your money?'

Bethany sighed. 'I don't know how much you intend to put in an appearance while I'm working at Portallen,' she said, 'but I'm making my own condition—that you don't mention Dan, his accident, and the compensation I received on his death. And, where possible, that you avoid passing fatuous remarks about the way I was hounded out of this village by gossip and innuendo. It's bad enough being here, Cavan,' she added, fixing him with a glare, 'without having you rub salt into the wound. OK?'

He nodded his agreement. 'I take it that means "yes". You won't regret the decision,' he said softly.

'I'm sure I won't, provided you keep your hands and your oyster satin sheets away from me.'

'I'll say this for you, Bethany,' he murmured, his voice betraying his admiration, 'you've got guts. And loyalty to your brother. You always did fuss over him like a replacement mother. But you must remember that he's a man now and you must let him make his own mistakes.'

'I don't need you to tell me that,' she said coldly. 'Just keep out of my hair.' Her eyes became cynical. 'I suppose Mawgan will see you as his benefactor.'

'I doubt it,' grinned Cavan, his eyes dancing wickedly. 'I intend to leave him in no doubt as to my opinion of him as a manager. I don't want to run the risk of him refusing my offer under the delusion that if he sacrificed his chance to paint he'd save you from a fate worse than death.'

'Tania won't be too pleased,' mused Bethany.

Cavan's grin broadened. 'Staked her claim, has she?' he enquired. When she ignored him, he glanced at his watch. 'Well, I suppose I must acquaint Mawgan with the facts of life and then, speaking of the facts of life, I ought to return to the yacht. Tania will probably have prepared a cordon-bleu supper for us.'

'She sounds a catch,' observed Bethany, trying to keep a casual smile on her face. And failing.

'She is,' smirked Cavan. 'A good all-rounder.' Bethany wondered if that included bed. Probably, she decided unhappily. Cavan wasn't the sort of man to kiss at the bedroom door, and Tania wasn't the sort of woman to let him, either. 'Trouble is,' he continued, 'she's so obviously out to land a millionaire this side of ninety that I can hear her tick coming a mile off.'

Bethany let out a laugh of delight before she recovered herself, ashamed that she'd laughed at her old friend. Cavan was looking at her in a strange, brooding way. 'What——' Her voice gave up, strangled into a croak by the dryness of her throat. He was walking towards her, and it was clear from his eyes, his sensual mouth, the animal prowl, what he intended to do. A parting gesture. Goodbye. A means of showing that he was now in control and dominating her.

She rose and backed against a wall, her palms flattened against it. He had come closer, his nostrils flaring, his eyes hypnotic. Anticipation set her on edge, her helplessness increasing with the drugging sensuality of his expression.

Gently Cavan took her head between the palms of his hands and gazed into her eyes, which had become the colour of soft Cornish rain. He leaned against her, the strength and vitality of his body almost overpowering her. Deliberately he shifted so that her body rubbed against his. He let out a low, throaty grunt, and she bit back her own sinful sigh which surged up.

Cavan's hot eyes were covered by his lowered lids as his long black lashes swept his cheeks and his head angled to kiss her.

'No!' she gasped.

'Why not?' he murmured huskily.

'Because you're bad news! Because I—I——'

His mouth was fuller and infinitely desirable. Bethany shrank against the wall, feeling the heavy thud of her heart echoing through her body. A wild desire arose inside her, the need to grab Cavan fiercely and draw his dark head down hard so that their kiss should blot out the world, the past, the future, and serve only as a rough, raw satisfaction for her eternal, remorseless hunger. Her body quivered with the effort of remaining cool and reluctant.

All she could do was plead with her eyes, for her protest emerged as small, plaintive noises in her throat which sounded alarmingly like urging demands of frustrated passion.

'Bethany,' he whispered. His breath flowed over her parted lips like a gentle sea breeze.

She hastily licked her mouth and tasted salt. His lips were irresistible and only a fraction away. She remembered the last time he'd kissed her, in full view of everyone in Fore Street—roughly, violently, flinging her from him in contempt. 'I don't want your damn blood money,' he'd roared, 'just your physical subjugation. Crawl, damn you, crawl!'

Bethany let out a groan of despair and turned her head to one side. Cavan must have thought it was a hoarse cry of need, for his mouth descended remorselessly on her throat, searching out the sweet hollow where her pulse hammered against her skin at the erotic touch of his lips, his probing tongue and his grazing, tormenting teeth.

'Cavan——' she husked in distress. She wanted him. She wanted to surrender.

'We'll take our time,' he murmured against her shoulder.

Bethany's eyes opened in alarm at the sensation of his lips moistly caressing her flesh. Her shoulder was bare. 'Time?' she cried harshly, trying to shrug her jacket back on. How had he managed to undo the buttons without her knowing? Oh, lord! she groaned inwardly. He was like a practised pickpocket whose hands could stray anywhere they chose with impunity. '*Time*?' she repeated in growing rage. 'You haven't lost much time in trying to strip me!'

'Mmm?' His head lifted, desire spilling from his eyes and making her legs infuriatingly weak. 'It just . . . sort of happened,' he explained, with a disarming grin. 'Gorgeous shoulders. Warm satin.'

Bethany raised her hand, and he stepped back quickly and stayed warily a short distance away from her, laughing. 'Don't you try that again!' she glowered.

'Can't promise,' he said, walking to the door as if she'd not really affected him at all. Bethany spluttered, muddled by the conflicting rage and longing which battled inside her treacherous body. 'I thought you said this turnkey business included everything?' he added insolently.

He'd slammed the door behind him, laughing merrily, before she had a chance to throw the teapot she'd picked up. Incensed, she banged it down and spent the next few minutes trying to clean tea from her expensive suit.

'Cavan Trevelyan,' she muttered grimly, sponging herself down, and wishing she could sponge away her need for him, 'you'll regret manhandling me as if I'm one of your popsies!'

CHAPTER THREE

TWENTY minutes later, Bethany had changed into her bathing costume, intending to cool herself down with a swim. She pulled on a pair of old cotton jeans and a loose T-shirt, slinging a towel around her neck, and strode briskly across the beach. Picking her way over the rocks and rock pools, she headed for Wrecker's Bay, the tiny cove tucked in the headland where there was a smart new coastguard station. As usual, the beach was deserted. She sat on her favourite flat rock and stared out to sea, stilling down her mind.

Cavan would be telling Mawgan now of the arrangement. Her face softened. She couldn't let Mawgan down. Of course she had to agree to Cavan's ultimatum. A few months here was no big deal. Bethany wrestled with her conscience and smiled wryly at her eagerness to convince herself that she could stay at Portallen, become involved with Cavan again—and not get hurt.

He'd always ended up hurting her. Even after her triumph in the end-of-term school play, when she'd spotted him at the back of the village hall, and had acted her heart out as the most convincing Juliet the drama teacher had ever known, Cavan had ruined her pleasure.

While everyone was congratulating her and she was smiling gently, wishing she could tell them that she had drawn her emotions from her own feelings, she'd been aware of Cavan's scornful eyes on her.

'What did you think of my performance, Cavan?' she'd finally blurted out, desperate for his admiration.

He had given her one cold look before turning on his heel. 'As a teenage seductress? *Alarmingly* practised,' he'd flung over his shoulder.

She had flushed scarlet, and the boys around her had sniggered knowingly.

Bethany lay back on the rock and closed her eyes, letting the late afternoon sun warm her body while she listened to the gentle wash of the waves. Her hand trailed idly in the clear water of a small rock pool as she tried to face her feelings honestly. Did she want Cavan because he was so completely unattainable? After all, he didn't like her, and merely saw her as a body he coveted, nothing more. Pure unfulfilled lust. Was it her vanity that kept urging her to try to captivate him?

She thought that perhaps Cavan had been right—that there were some people who just *had* to master everything and everyone they came across. He was definitely one of those people; maybe she was, too.

It was ironic. He kept making a play for her despite his unconcealed contempt, because she was apparently indifferent to him. His masculine pride was offended by her evasion. She secretly longed for Cavan—maybe for the same reason. She grinned ruefully. She was being incredibly juvenile, and ought to scurry off to Bodmin at once. And yet...

She found herself beaming, blissfully content now that she was back in Portallen. Unnerving though it would be, working with Cavan, it might be a good discipline professionally. She *had* lost touch with the design world, and had also lost much of her self-confidence. Doing this job might give her the assurance to summon up the nerve to work in London, and later, perhaps, to set up her own business.

There was another benefit. By owning half of Portallen, she'd have an excuse to come here now and again, rationing herself, of course, to the occasions when Cavan wasn't around.

One of her fingers came into contact with a sea anemone, which gently captured the finger, sucking it in with its tentacles. Afraid of damaging it, she waited till it had discovered it didn't want to devour her and let her go. Shaking her wet hand and sitting up, she began to plan.

Cavan wouldn't stay for long; he didn't like the country life. He'd left Portallen for London the moment he'd saved up enough for the train fare, shortly before his seventeenth birthday. Reassured by that thought, she lay back again, imagining brief holiday visits when Mawgan returned on weekends, full of his activities at the art college . . .

'If you're doing sit-ups, that's only two in the last five minutes.'

Bethany kept her eyes resolutely closed on hearing Cavan's voice. 'I came here to get away from you,' she retorted with a slight frown.

'Failed again,' he said cheerfully.

She heard a rustle and then felt his body close to hers. Every inch of her tingled. It was as if he'd flicked on a powerful generator inside her, she thought resentfully, and lit up all her lights.

'Please, Cavan,' she said in a reasonable tone. 'I need personal space. I've been used to isolation. It's been a long time since I lived with anyone——'

'Really? No man on the moors with you?' he enquired smoothly. 'Not even a toy boy, perhaps?'

'No. Don't you mellow with age? You must be thirty now. Time you curbed your belligerence,' she rebuked. A warm, firm finger traced the line between her brows, and she quivered.

'I was only asking a question. I am your stepbrother. I'm interested in what's been happening to you over the past two years,' he said quietly.

'I've had no relationships,' she said flatly. 'I've lived a very private life.'

'You turned in on yourself.' It was a statement, not a question, and she didn't confirm it, feeling a little disconcerted by the unusually thoughtful-sounding Cavan. She was dying to open her eyes and see his expression. 'I'm not surprised; you must have been a fish out of water up there. You don't belong on the open moorland. You looked happy, lying on the rock,' he observed perceptively. 'There's something here that holds you, isn't there? It holds me too.'

Bethany peeked through her lashes. He was staring at the distant horizon, a look of intense longing on his face that made her throat catch. He'd changed into jeans and a white open-neck shirt which made the most of his mountain-range chest and what looked like a Caribbean tan, judging by his deep-gold throat and forearms. She sat up and wilted under the glorious smile he gave her. It was like being gently sucked in by the sea anemone.

'Once upon a time Portallen *was* perfect,' she mused, a little irritated with herself because she wanted to reach out and touch him. And be captured. But then, she'd only be spat out again after a brief, exploratory period. 'Mawgan and I had an idyllic childhood.'

'And then I came along,' he said softly. 'The fairy-tale turned into a different kind of story. The minute our eyes met, straight away a tempest blew up.'

Her face sobered. 'You made my life hell——'

Cavan's sharp inhalation interrupted her. 'Mutual,' he said with a low savagery. 'I could hardly breathe in that house without your eyes on me. If Mother hadn't been so much in love... Bethany, you do know how happy your father was with my mother, don't you?'

'Yes,' she said reluctantly. 'He was nuts about her. But you ruined it all by arguing with him constantly——'

Cavan shrugged. 'I'd never had a father. I'd been my own man for years. I was sixteen and street-wise, Beth! It was hard being told what to do and what not to do. Your father was used to Mawgan's quiet obedience, not an adolescent stepson who prowled around where and when he liked.'

'All those girls!' recalled Bethany with faint distaste. Girls from the village, from Polperro, Looe, Liskeard and Plymouth, then London—she'd been able to trace Cavan's wanderings by where the girls came from.

A blissful look came over Cavan's face, and Bethany felt the humiliating pangs of jealousy. 'It was wonderful! I was in and out of love more often than a kid's fingers in a bag of chips,' he said with a low, husky laugh.

Bethany's breathing shortened, her breasts rising and falling quickly. It distressed her to remember those girls— all ages, sizes, but all beautiful and all madly in love with Cavan.

'Father was worried sick about your morals and whether you'd get any of the girls into trouble,' she said stiffly—and then wanted to take the priggish words back.

Cavan smiled. 'No, he wasn't. Not for long. He had no need—I assured him of that. I never risked hurting them.' His eyebrows lifted. 'You don't look as if you believe me.'

'No. I heard a different story from them,' she said, remembering the tears, the pleas for her intercession, the hints that Cavan had taken what he wanted and ditched them.

'Ah, but Bethany, you know how gossip distorts the truth, how lies can be spread,' he pointed out gently. 'Women can be very proud. Try not to believe everything you hear about me.'

'If I believed half, I'd be wary of you.'

'Ditto.'

Bethany bristled. 'What do you mean by that?'

'Your father was much more concerned about you than he was about me.'

She turned her head slowly to meet his serious eyes. 'Whatever for?' she asked in surprise.

'Anyone could see you were a hothouse flower in a bed of dandelions,' he smiled ruefully. 'We all knew you'd spread your wings one day. We——' Cavan avoided her eyes, as if changing his mind about what he'd intended to say, and he glanced up to scowl at the cloud which was obscuring the sun. 'He was very upset when you left home to marry Dan. You were very young.'

'You don't know what I was like at the age of eighteen,' she retorted. 'You were working in the nightclub in the West End.' And, judging by the joy in his face when she'd seen him shortly before she decided to marry Dan, he'd been perfectly happy there, living the sophisticated life of the big city. She'd felt very provincial beside him in his smart suit and with his smart talk. Particularly she'd felt humiliated by a rather patronising woman he'd brought down to stay. Some hotel receptionist.

Portallen had lost him and so had she. The familiar haunts cruelly reminded her of that loss. In addition, Rosie and her father had innocently hurt her with their public displays of warm, tender affection because she knew she'd never feel such passion for anyone other than the callous Cavan. That was when Bethany had impulsively agreed to marry the persistent Dan, who had promised her his love and an escape from the house which held such painful memories.

'I knew you, nevertheless,' he said, his eyes piercingly blue. 'Every inch.' Bethany's breath was suddenly trapped in her lungs. The back of her neck tightened at the way his eyes were roaming over her body. 'I'd know your body and your voice and your perfume in a room of a hundred people. I knew then that you weren't ready for marriage.' He gave her a speculative look. 'Perhaps you are now.'

She gathered her wits together. 'You couldn't be more wrong. Men are a turn-off for me,' she said pointedly.

'Oh? When did your tastes change so drastically?' he countered. Bethany gave him a withering stare and half rose, but he pulled her down again. 'Dan?' he suggested in a hard tone. 'You've convinced yourself that you're pining?'

'You don't pull your punches, do you?' she muttered.

He grunted. 'I want to know. I'm not much good at pussyfooting around.'

Bethany's mouth twisted into a wry smile. He'd always plunged straight for the jugular, and she'd always lunged straight back in defence. 'Look,' she said, trying to be reasonable, 'what happened to me was extremely painful and traumatic. I'm still getting over it. I'll *never* put it behind me.'

'You must,' he frowned.

'Why? After all, *you* can't even forget or forgive my attempts to put down an arrogant, overbearing, bullying stepbrother. Why should I forget the man I was married to and the nightmare events after his death?'

'Because you're alive!' he growled, gripping her arm fiercely. 'Alive and young and beautiful. And aching for the things that no man has yet given you.'

Bethany's jaw dropped open. 'Aching? My God, Cavan! Words fail me! Just because you think of nothing else, you needn't imagine sex is on everyone else's minds.'

'You think I'm talking about sex?' he asked huskily.

She flung her head back in exasperation, her body taut and proud. 'What else do you ever think about?' she scathed. Cavan's lashes fluttered a fraction. 'In your narrow and limited imagination you have pictured me, rich and lonely, sitting alone on Bodmin moor, and have smugly come to the conclusion that I need a man! Really! Of all the chauvinistic——'

'It's you who are obsessed with sex,' he said shortly. 'You were deliberately provocative as a teenager. Even now every movement of your body is designed to enslave any man who happens to be around.' Bethany saw that there was a glittering light in his eyes, one which warned her that his desire to master her physically was very strong. 'I have to admit, I'm tempted. Every time you move, every time you speak,' he murmured.

She quivered throughout her responsive body. 'Don't pester me, Cavan,' she complained in a low voice.

'You never loved Dan,' he continued relentlessly. 'You were just running away from life.'

'It was hardly running away. I travelled the world,' she insisted.

'You don't have to go further than your front door to live deeply,' said Cavan huskily. 'And when you returned to Portallen, after Dan died, I knew by merely glancing at you that you were untouched inside. Own up, Bethany,' he demanded roughly. 'Wild passion wasn't a feature of your marriage.'

She kept her mouth firmly shut, ignoring him. Because he was right. She and Dan had enjoyed being together, but it had all been on the surface. They were apart for long periods and when he was on leave they seemed to be forever having parties. There was no deep relationship. How could there be?

'Have you no consideration for my feelings? I asked you not to talk about Dan,' she said eventually in a shaky whisper.

'I know. But I feel that until you come to terms with the truth of those feelings you'll never be free of the past. You're pretending to yourself you loved him to salve your conscience for accepting all that money.'

Bethany drew in a harsh, ragged breath and jumped up. 'You think you can play me on a line till I'm exhausted. You think you can hook me, chalk me up on your achievement board and throw me back in the sea!' she cried, her huge sea-storm eyes betraying her distress. 'Well, you're wrong. I've learnt the hard way to be tough inside. Life's smashed me down but I'm coming back up, and I won't let you destroy my confidence. I'll work for you because I have to, because I want Portallen. But that's *it*.'

He stood, his body blocking out the late afternoon sun. '*Now* you've woken up. You're going to live again. Thank God! I thought you'd lost your fire.' His eyes brooded on her. 'You know there's something unfinished between us,' he said huskily.

His face was shadowed, but it seemed to Bethany that his eyes carried a blazing message of need. Her mind fought; her body began to surrender. There was a melting note in his voice which was infinitely seductive, and she felt the magnetism between them pulling her inexorably towards him.

'No, Cavan,' she mumbled almost incoherently. She concentrated on holding herself erect, preventing her body from swaying towards him as it wanted to.

'Bethany,' he whispered, 'we want each other. You can't deny that. It's a primitive urge that has nothing to do with common sense. This heat, this... burning, the extraordinary excitement that's generated between us——'

She had clenched her teeth, refusing to acknowledge that he'd put her own feelings into words. And so she lied to him. 'Primitive?' she echoed, faint scorn in her voice. 'Heat? Oh, come on, Cavan! You've been watching too many bad films.'

He shrugged. 'I just said what I felt. I was never much good with the flowery words,' he said, all defenceless innocence.

Despite herself, Bethany's heart jerked. 'You were never much good, period,' she said defensively.

His eyes suddenly lost their helpless look and became unnervingly sultry. 'Wrong. I was always very good,' he said in a husky voice. 'And still am. You'll find that out soon, or——'

'Or your name's not really Trevelyan?' she finished for him defiantly.

Cavan roared with outright laughter. 'I like it! I adore you, Bethany,' he murmured. 'You fight me, you kick and struggle, you make me laugh. Life's never boring when you're around.'

The tension had been broken. And Bethany felt a contrary disappointment and a sense of loss. 'Wish I could say the same for you,' she said crossly, turning her back on him.

It had been a mistake. She sensed his arms coming around her. In a flash she had deftly slipped out of them and was up off the rock and running, caution and cowardice overcoming her pride. He looked too sure of his strength to hold her a prisoner in those powerful arms of his, and too darn set on bending her to his will for her to take any chances. Better to lose her dignity, she thought breathlessly, as she pounded over the sand with a laughing Cavan in hot pursuit, than to have her mouth and body ravaged by his roaming lips and hands.

'You...tease...me...Bethany...Trevelyan,' he yelled, 'and you'll...regret it!'

She whirled, and he stopped some yards away, grinning at her. 'This isn't a tease! I was running away from you! It isn't a "come-on",' she protested vehemently.

Bethany realised that she couldn't get around the headland because the tide was almost up over the rocks. And Cavan barred the way back to the main beach. All that was left was a choice of clambering up the sheer cliff, or escaping via the sea. Waves were lapping at her feet, even now. Uncertainly, she turned to face him, watching him warily, both of them up to their ankles in the white surf.

'Old films... bit like *From Here to Eternity*, isn't it?' he said triumphantly, his teeth flashing in his dark face like a predatory shark's.

Worrying about any possible connection between the steamy love-scene in the surf in that film and Cavan's intentions, Bethany folded her arms across her chest in defence and focused her attention pointedly on the perfect white teeth.

'More like *Jaws II*,' she retorted, trying to deflate him.

His dark eyebrow crooked high. 'Do you think so? Didn't the shark win in that film?' he enquired, wide-eyed and disarming.

'Oh, leave me alone!' she said in desperation.

His eyes narrowed. He studied her closely for a while, and then nodded slowly. 'All right. I will—for now. It's early days yet, and we have all the time in the world.'

'Until Christmas,' she reminded him quickly.

He smiled, and she felt a beat of fear in her throat. 'I don't need that long. I'll catch you when you least expect it. Don't be misled into thinking that I've given up. I never do that. I've wanted you for as long as I can remember. Until I have you, I'll never know whether you've been worth the wait or are merely a totally illogical craving.' He began to walk away and then spun on his heel to face her again, looking rougher and tougher than she'd ever known. 'Anticipation is sweet,' he growled, 'but I believe that making love to you will be sweeter.'

'You'll never know,' she said, alarmed to hear how husky her voice had become from panic at his threat. Her lips parted softly and she looked at him warily from under her lashes.

'You bitch! You are teasing me! A real man-tormentor, aren't you?' He paused, his chest heaving. '*Alarmingly* practised,' he grated.

He strode towards her, and she found to her dismay that she couldn't move. There was such anger in his face that she was terrified. He yanked her into his hard, unyielding body and kissed her brutally, his mouth forcing down on hers, his arms crushing the breath from her. And then he had pushed her contemptuously away and had abandoned her, with the waves breaking over her ankles, undermining the sand beneath her feet so that she rocked unsteadily.

Bethany felt a moan wrench from deep within her chest. The kiss had made him even angrier; she could tell that from the set of his high shoulders as he walked across the beach. For her, the kiss had taken away some of her explosive energy, but not enough of it.

She waited till he'd become a small, distant figure on the stone jetty on the other side of the bay and then she strode back above the high-tide level. Methodically she began to remove her clothes. In her old blue bathing costume, she ran down to the sea. It was freezing, but she needed to exhaust herself physically. She needed the cold shock to clear her mind and to chill down her reluctantly awoken body.

Stony-faced, she waded through the coldly slapping waves, her feet like ice. With a sudden lunge, she dived in and came up breathless with the cold. Her eyes lifted, drawn helplessly to the figure on the jetty. Cavan was apparently watching her and gesturing for her to come out of the sea.

Of course she defied him—she couldn't have him dictating to her. She'd have a quick swim to show Cavan that she wasn't going to leap to his bidding whenever he snapped his fingers, but she wouldn't stay in for long. Recklessly she struck out for the open sea, quickly finding all her old swimming skills returning, and suddenly she felt as if she'd been born in the water. Exhilarated by the discovery, she abandoned her mind to the rhythm of the fast crawl.

And then she felt an agonising pain in her calf and she disappeared beneath the water in a flurry of flailing arms and legs. Her head surfaced briefly.

'*Cavan*!' she screamed. She raised an arm in a desperate signal before the cramp paralysed her again and she sank like a stone, the dark water no longer friendly and welcoming but terrifying. Cavan, she thought. *Cavan*.

Had he been watching? Or...?

Her head was bursting. She clenched her teeth and kicked strongly so that she shot to the surface. She floundered for a while, trying to stay afloat despite the vicious pain in her calf. She could see the grey bulk of the Portallen Inn, the uninhabited jetty. Cavan had gone. Despair racked her.

'Cavan!' she sobbed hopelessly.

'Hold on! For God's sake, Beth, hold on! Keep shouting; I can hardly see you.'

His voice had come thinly over the waves, above the sound of an outboard engine. She yelled, dipped below the surface and swallowed sea-water. Suddenly a huge, welcome hand grabbed her shoulder in a grip of steel. Half fainting with fear, she caught a brief glimpse of Cavan's dark, alarmed face leaning from a boat, before she slipped from his grasp and the agonising cramp doubled her up, rolling her in a tangled ball beneath the waves again.

He must have dived in immediately because his body cannoned into hers, drawing her upwards, and she joyously abandoned herself to him, wrapping her arms around his neck and curling her legs around his waist.

'Beth! *Beth*! Open your eyes! God...!'

She choked. Felt his hands unravelling her arms and legs and turning her around.

'Grab the boat!' he cried in her ear.

Bethany felt the hard wood slam into her ribs as he thrust her upwards out of the water. 'I can't!' she gasped.

'You damn well can!' he roared, giving her an almighty shove.

She tumbled into the boat, hitting her head on the seat and lying in stunned relief, aware that the boat was rocking violently as Cavan clambered in too. And then she was in his arms, the water falling from his clothes in a silver shower. She didn't protest. This wasn't the moment. All she cared about was that she was alive and he was holding her and he couldn't see her expression so she could enjoy every second.

She shivered, and he clasped her closer till she could feel the thunderous beat of his heart from his recent exertion. 'My God, Bethany,' he cried hoarsely, huge gasps of breath tearing his body, 'I thought I'd never see you again!'

'What?' she mumbled in confusion. She must have misheard what he'd said. There was a roaring in her ears. She pushed him away slightly and passed her hand over her head. Her fingers felt sticky.

'You're hurt,' he said gently. Delicate fingers felt her brow, and then she thought she felt his lips there. 'We've got to get you back,' he told her reluctantly, his eyes melting into hers.

'Yes,' she whispered. Her hands flattened in wonder and pleasure against his torso. Beneath his saturated shirt, she could feel the outline of every strongly defined muscle. 'You are soaked to the skin,' she said stupidly.

'And you.'

His husky voice made her look up, and then she followed his gaze to her own breasts, their shape beneath the wet costume leaving nothing at all to the imagination. She blushed, still shaken, still blissfully relieved that she was alive. Suddenly she felt that anything was possible. Even discovering that Cavan had emotions somewhere beneath that tough-guy exterior. The brief moments of danger had put everything into proportion. She cuddled into him, utterly thankful.

'Oh, Cavan!' she sighed, before she could stop herself.

'Hell!' he growled.

His mouth covered hers, warm as the sun, sweet as honey and as potent as barrel cider. Before she could catch her breath, he kissed her again and her arms seemed to float up to link in his wet black hair. Then he slid her slowly to the bottom of the boat, covering her with his body as if to keep it warm, and she revelled in every exquisite second of the movement, allowing herself to go along with his pretence.

'Are you all right?' he murmured softly.

'I am now. I was frightened,' she croaked, excusing herself for not pushing him away.

'Shh. I'm here now. You're safe.' His mouth roamed over her jawline while his hands involuntarily ran up to her breasts. When they touched each firm peak, she inhaled sharply at the shock which ran through her and which deepened the terrible ache in her loins. He frowned. 'I didn't mean to touch you... Oh, Bethany!' he groaned.

With difficulty, she fought her way out of the deep water she seemed to have got herself in. Confused, she tried to understand why he should be so shaken by touching her breasts and by her give-away reaction. Astonishingly, she did feel safe with him—why, she had no idea.

'Frightened,' she mumbled. 'I had cramp... oh!' Her rambling was interrupted by the spear of pleasure coursing through her, created by Cavan's delicate fingers caressing her hardening nipples. Despite her intentions, her head had tipped back at the glorious sensation and her eyes had closed. All she could hear was Cavan's heavy breathing, all she could smell was the sea-water on his body.

'I ought to be getting you to shore,' he said huskily.

'Yes. Oh! Please... don't... Cavan!' she jerked out, protesting half-heartedly. She was now fully aware of what she *should* be saying and doing, and was wishing fervently that she didn't have to deny herself what she wanted so very much.

Cavan's fingers were driving her crazy, his tender kisses and gentle murmurings arousing her senses. He drew back a little and his bemused eyes searched hers. With a smile, he bent and kissed her full on the mouth, his tongue lightly stroking her upper lip.

'Enough,' he growled throatily. He raised himself, looking puzzled. 'God! What am I thinking of? I'm sorry. I lost my head. We can't stay out here. You'll get pneumonia. Bethany, I know you're a superb swimmer. You had cramp, you say? Has it gone or shall I massage your leg?'

'It's gone.' Her wet-lashed eyes were fixed on him, and she saw his expression become cautious. He held out his hand, and there was an impassivity about his features suddenly as if he wanted to hide his thoughts.

'You'd better sit up and cuddle into me,' he said gruffly.

Without another word, he hauled her up and drew her to the stern of the dinghy, where he tucked her into him and started the outboard engine. Crushed against his chest, she wondered what had stopped him from taking advantage of her. It wouldn't have been *that* difficult, she thought ruefully. Perhaps he was cold. His hand lightly stroked the bump on her forehead and she began to wonder if Cavan was quite as heartless as he made out.

'Throw yer line, boy.'

Bethany lifted her head from its warm shelter, and saw to her dismay that several fishermen were waiting on the jetty steps. They pulled in the dinghy and Cavan lifted her in his arms, his face inscrutable. Jory Pengelly's face appeared in her line of vision, and she felt the heavy weight of his fishy-smelling cable-knit sweater being wrapped around her.

'All right, boy?' asked Jory, when Cavan stumbled slightly on the slippery step.

'Shaky,' he admitted in his gravelly voice. 'I thought she was a goner.'

'You saved my life,' whispered Bethany, staring up at him.

Tiny drops of water pattered down on her face from Cavan's black hair. He looked rather vulnerable when his eyes met hers, and then they slid away and he increased his pace, striding towards the hotel ahead of the fascinated men, his gaze firmly ahead.

'I know. I have plans for it,' he said to her softly. 'I'm damned if I'm letting such a gorgeous body feed the fishes. I want my share first.'

She slumped limply in his arms, her wistful dreams dashed. For a moment, in her stupid, dazed condition, she'd thought he had been genuinely concerned for her.

'Put me down!' she mumbled miserably. 'Put me *down*!' Surprised, he stopped and set her on her feet, steadying her when she swayed. 'I'm caught between the devil and the deep blue sea,' she husked. 'What a choice I have!' Stumbling blindly, hearing the astonished murmur of the men behind her, she made her way into the hall and collapsed on the floor.

The door slammed, rattling the windows as Cavan stormed in. 'You stupid, impetuous, stubborn... Oh, Bethany! You deserve a thrashing!' said Cavan in exasperation, his soaking-wet socks coming into view. His hands reached down and slipped them off so that he was barefoot, and then he had picked her up again and was carrying her upstairs to her room.

'You put me down!' she ordered, her lips trembling.

He ignored her. 'Going out there for a swim! It was freezing,' he muttered. 'You still behave like a stubborn kid sometimes, don't you? I suppose you saw me beckoning you to come in, and decided to show me who was boss. Sometimes you make me so mad that I really want to teach you a lesson!'

Without any gentleness, he threw her on the bed, where she bounced. Before she could scramble away, warned to make the attempt by his threatening expression, he had yanked away the warm sweater and his hands were pulling on the straps of her bathing costume.

'No!' she cried, her eyes enormous.

To her utter humiliation, he ripped it down expertly as if he'd been stripping women all his life. She tensed her muscles in fear, but he kept his glittering eyes fixed relentlessly on hers. 'Are you expecting rape?' he seethed.

Her hands covered her body as she struggled to speak. 'Don't,' she breathed in terror.

'God!' he ground out through his teeth. Brutally he rolled her in the duvet. Half hidden, her startled face peeped out at him in astonishment. 'You've got a low opinion of me, haven't you? Don't you dare move. I'll bring a plaster for your head and some soup for your stomach and then I'll go and give myself a massive slug of whisky for my reward,' he said savagely.

She watched him stride to the door, feeling miserable and contrite because she'd misjudged him. He was angry because he'd had to rescue her and had got his clothes wet, with little thanks at the end.

'Cavan!' she croaked. 'Wait! I thought…I thought…'

He stopped, his back to her. 'I know what you thought, Bethany,' he muttered grimly. 'I had no idea you held me in such contempt.'

'I—I am grateful,' she managed, her heart pounding. 'If it weren't for you, I might be dead.'

'Yes. Possibly. Therefore you owe me a debt of gratitude,' he said. His head jerked around and he scowled at her. 'And now I know where I stand in your estimation, I'll make damn sure I collect,' he said with soft menace. 'But not until you're fully aware of what I'm doing.' Bethany swallowed. 'Oh, God!' he whispered, and strode quickly through the doorway.

She cuddled into the duvet, feeling her chilled body slowly returning to normal. Which was more than she could say of her turbulent emotions.

CHAPTER FOUR

MAWGAN, at least, was blissfully, radiantly happy. He spent the next few days sorting everything he'd need in case he did manage to get a place in art college that year. Bethany sat on the quayside one evening, enjoying the sunset and thinking of her rescue. Cavan had been gentle with her, she mused. With a woman he could trust, he'd be very caring.

'None the worse fer wear, then?'

She turned her head slightly and smiled hopefully at Jory. It was the first time anyone in the village had voluntarily spoken to her. 'I'm fine, thanks to Cavan.'

'Aye. Good man, that.'

Her mouth dropped open in amazement. They disliked him, surely! 'He was very brave,' she said uncertainly.

'No,' scoffed Jory. 'It weren't nothin' to Cavan. Saw him pick two kids off a lilo near Tallen Point last year in worse seas than that.' Jory scrutinised her carefully. 'Goin' home soon?' he asked slyly.

'I am home, Jory,' she answered evenly, meeting his hostile eyes with a start. 'I'm staying for a while,' she added defiantly.

'Yeah. Tania said.' He looked over to a group of his friends some yards away. To Bethany they looked faintly threatening, the way they were staring at her with hard, cold expressions on their faces. 'Don't take a hint, do you, girl?'

Her pulses quickened and she tried not to look scared. 'I hadn't noticed one,' she replied pleasantly.

'You're not welcome here,' said Jory impassively.

'What do you——?' She stopped in mid-sentence and heaved a sigh of angry frustration. Jory had stalked off, evidently telling his mates what he'd said because they kept looking back and laughing. It hadn't ended, then. It was just beginning. She wondered how long she'd be able to stand it.

'Beth!'

She hastily rearranged her face and managed a smile when Mawgan came running down to see her, his face lit up with excitement. 'What's happened?' she asked affectionately.

'Cavan phoned! He's got me an interview at the art college for tomorrow,' cried Mawgan, his eyes shining. 'How, I don't know—I would have thought they were full, but there's one place free. Anyway, you know Cavan; he doesn't let anything stand in his way when he sets his mind on something.'

'That's true,' she agreed with a wry laugh. 'I'm thrilled,' she said, giving him a hug and putting aside her anxiety about Jory's attitude. 'One place. What luck,' she said slowly, wondering if that was a coincidence.

'If I'm accepted, I can start at the end of next week, since there aren't any more visitors coming here,' continued Mawgan enthusiastically. 'And he's found me a flat near the college through some contacts. He doesn't let the dust settle when he gets started. Isn't Cavan amazing?'

That, thought Bethany, was no coincidence. Cavan had planned the whole thing some time ago, she was certain. 'Don't forget that he'll own a bit of you,' she pointed out, reluctant to dampen Mawgan's excitement but even more reluctant to acknowledge that Cavan was amazing. 'He *is* going to take a percentage of your future earnings.'

'It's not much return for his money. He deserves a reasonable return for his investment. It'll cost him thousands. I'm determined not to let him down. I'm going to be a success for all our sakes, believe me.'

'I know you will,' said Bethany warmly. It was ironic. Stubborn Cornish pride had made Mawgan refuse her offer of the compensation money. But now Cavan had succeeded where she'd failed. By tying the allowance to a strictly business deal, Cavan had ensured that Mawgan kept his self-respect. He'd motivated Mawgan, too, knowing her brother would consider it a matter of honour to work hard and justify the financial investment.

Cavan knew her brother better than she did. She chewed her lip, considering the implications. Far from being blunt and direct, Cavan was showing a clever and rather devious mind. But then, any man who rose from being a bell-boy to running a multi-million pound ticket agency couldn't exactly be a slouch. He had a sharp mind, and it would be stupid of her to underestimate his ability to manipulate situations and people to his advantage. She must be on her guard all the time.

'Beth?' Mawgan was giving her arm a shake. 'You're not listening!' he said, hurt.

'Sorry,' she smiled in apology. 'I was thinking of what lies ahead.' She shivered, feeling Cavan's tentacles closing in around her. He was getting his own way too frequently. 'I'm going in. It's getting cold.'

As she ran up the stairs, she thought angrily that this time she'd make sure Cavan didn't get everything he wanted. He could relieve his appetite with Tania. Her mouth turned down at the idea and she stopped short with a silent groan. Jealousy again, and quite illogical of her.

Showering hastily and dressing in a thin cream wool dress for the cooler evening, Bethany slipped downstairs and found Mawgan rushing about in the kitchen like a demented thing, preparing supper.

'Chef's off sick,' he said tersely. 'Phoned in ten minutes ago.'

'I'll help.' Bethany had intended to borrow his car and find a quiet pub somewhere to spend the evening, but hadn't the heart to leave him in the midst of such chaos. She grabbed an apron and commandeered the grill-pan.

'You'll be all right when I go, won't you?' asked Mawgan, prodding the broccoli. 'Cavan will be here now and then.'

She decided not to tell him about Jory. 'Mmm.' She tried to be non-committal. She didn't want Mawgan worrying.

'I know you two will get on,' he said earnestly. 'All that arguing—it's only a front. You've got the wrong idea about each other, you know. He isn't some Neanderthal tribesman, trying to drag you into his cave.'

'Then he shouldn't keep trying to do his impression of one,' she frowned. 'I thought you'd always loathed him?'

'No, Beth.' Mawgan swung her around and held her shoulders. 'You did. You were my mother, my sister, my friend. You flared up like a torch whenever he was around, and I adored you so I backed you up. We didn't give him much of a welcome. Look at it from his point of view; he was like a fish out of water. Remember how he learnt to sail?'

She grinned. 'Don't we all! Cavan fell in so many times you said he'd get webbed feet.' Her grin faded. Exhausted, wet and laughed at by the local boys, Cavan had persevered through the day till darkness fell. And eventually he had mastered the art of dinghy-sailing so well that he became more skilled than anyone. Nothing beat him. Not ever. Her face became very thoughtful.

'He's a tough nut,' smiled Mawgan. 'You've got to admire his guts. Give him a chance, for my sake.'

'He pulled me out of the sea, and of course I'll always be grateful. But it doesn't mean I have to like him.'

Mawgan shrugged and went to turn over the roast potatoes. His eyes slid over to his sister's pensive face. 'He rang from the yacht. Tania was doing some exotic dinner. Lobster and profiteroles,' he said. 'Candle-light. Very romantic, with Tania in some slinky number. Hasn't she altered? I could hardly believe my eyes. Fancy having her as a secretary!' he laughed. 'What do you think of her?' he asked idly.

'I think they're perfect for each other,' she said ferociously, spearing the chops and turning them over.

'It's a cosy arrangement,' mused Mawgan. 'She's really landed on her feet. Flying all round the world together... Thrown together like that, they must be quite close——'

Bethany banged the grill-pan back, her face stormy. 'I wouldn't know and I wouldn't *care*,' she said, quickly interrupting him. She didn't like the images he was conjuring up. Cavan kissing Tania. Tania's fluttery lashes... 'What else can I do for you?' she asked sharply.

Mawgan smiled. 'Not much,' he said, holding back a grin. 'I think I have the situation sussed.'

Bethany luxuriated in bed. It was Sunday, and all the visitors had left. Mawgan had gone too, his car laden with his possessions, an ecstatic smile on his face. Tomorrow she'd start work, so this would be her last lazy day. Contentedly, she plumped up her pillows and reached for a magazine.

Her hand froze in mid-air. The door-handle of her room was turning. Bethany clutched a pillow defensively. She was alone in the house. No one was within earshot.

'Who's there?' she called sharply, her voice shaking slightly. 'Mawgan?'

The door swung open to reveal . . . nothing. Bethany stared at the empty corridor, her head cocked to one side in a listening attitude, her breath shallow and high in her throat. Then she blinked. Around the side of the door appeared a fishing-line, on the end of which dangled a child's inflatable shark.

Her relief was intense. 'Cavan! I know that's you— no one else would be so stupidly childish. What are you playing at? Come out! Are you trying to scare me?'

'Peace offering.' The shark jiggled appealingly, its toothy smile and huge eyes suddenly making her want to laugh.

'*Peace* offering?' she repeated in surprise. A sou'wester hat was thrown into the room followed by an enormous bunch of parsley, a lemon and finally a spade. A spade?

Despite herself, Bethany began to giggle uncontrollably, laughing so much at the ridiculous objects that she was clutching herself weakly and lying back on the pillows when Cavan finally peeked around the doorway.

'Can I come in and do penance?' he enquired hopefully.

'To the door only.' Still grinning, Bethany took the precaution of sliding beneath the duvet a little even if he didn't look in the least bit threatening.

He beamed, ignoring her request and coming in to stand humbly at the bottom of her bed. She managed to wipe her eyes and made a brave attempt at composing herself. '*Parsley*?' she queried. 'Shouldn't it be flowers?'

'Oh. Clumsy me,' he said disarmingly, pushing a hand through his tumbled hair. 'I suppose "say it with parsley" doesn't have the same glamour,' he apologised. 'But, being a practical and unromantic man, I thought roses wouldn't go with fish.'

He was far too appealing for his own good. 'They don't. Neither does the spade,' she said drily, dying to know the connection and wondering ruefully how many women he'd *laughed* into bed.

'We need the spade. To bury the hatchet,' he explained. Bethany sternly suppressed another giggle, but her mouth twitched, giving her away. 'It's nice to hear you laugh,' Cavan said contentedly. 'It's been a long time, Bethany.'

Her amusement faded abruptly, and she thought for a moment 'It has,' she agreed in wonder. 'Ages.' She refrained from telling him when. The last time she'd been totally helpless with laughter was when Cavan had played the Ugly Sister in the village pantomime, sporting a pair of yellow wellies and a hairy chest above an enormous bosom which kept slipping and being ostentatiously adjusted, with a wicked wink from his amazing false eyelashes. She found that she was smiling at the memory, and sighed.

Cavan had been watching her. 'Am I forgiven?' he asked quietly.

'It depends what for.'

'Coming on strong on the beach,' he said bluntly. 'I realise that was probably why you went for a swim. You needed to release your anger with me. I'm sorry. I didn't want to put you in danger like that. To tell the truth, I was rather wound up.'

'And now?' she asked uncertainly, wondering if the romantic dinner with Tania had unwound him. 'You made a threat before you left. Do you intend to carry it out?'

'You come straight to the point, don't you?' he said ruefully.

'Well, I think I'd better let you know that if you try anything on I'll report you for harassment,' she warned him. 'I'd be working for you so I'd be legally entitled to protest. You must see that I won't get much work done if I'm spending half my time dodging your great groping paws.'

'I know,' he said amiably, giving in with surprising alacrity. 'And I want everything finished ... It'll have to be Ticking Tania, won't it?'

Bethany met his laughing eyes and her mouth curled up in delight at the nickname before she managed to control its waywardness and look prim again. But Cavan was laughing his wicked laugh, and his wrecker's eyes were flashing merrily at her, and she became convulsed with giggles once more.

'You are quite the most infuriating man I've ever met,' she protested eventually.

'Aren't I just?' His eyes glowed and he sat down on the bed. Immediately alert for danger, Bethany resisted the urge to shrink back, and gave him a challenging stare instead. He leaned forwards, his mouth soft, and she wanted to touch it. 'I'll tell you this, Bethany,' he said huskily. 'You're going to love every second of the next half-hour.' He let his tongue slick over his lips and his gaze roamed slowly over the length of her body, which was outlined beneath the thin summer duvet.

She snatched up the bedside lamp and waved it threateningly. 'That does it!' she said crossly, disappointed in him. 'You promised——'

'Don't you want the breakfast I've cooked?' he asked with hurt innocence. 'Local home-cured bacon, local eggs, field mushrooms from the headland and your own tomatoes?'

She became aware of the glorious smell coming from downstairs, and replaced the lamp very carefully, giving herself time to let her annoyance subside. He'd been teasing her as usual. Like an annoying older brother, endlessly teasing his sister. Irritated, she surveyed him from under her eyebrows, wondering if that was how he saw her, and if that was why he tormented her so relentlessly.

'One of these days, Cavan, you'll get your come-uppance,' she promised wryly. 'I'll get the better of you, see if I don't!'

'Sounds fun,' he grinned. 'I love masterful women.'

'No, you don't. You hate them. You ache to crush them and assert your masculinity.' Bethany tore her eyes away from his and sought for normality. 'Breakfast,' she said briskly. 'I'm starving.'

'Chew on Jaws here till you can make it downstairs,' he suggested, getting up and tossing her the toy shark. She caught it and eyed him with reluctant amusement. 'Two minutes, and breakfast will be on the table, ready or not,' he said smugly.

'Two——!' Compressing her mouth, she grabbed her nail scissors from the bedside table and stabbed Jaws. The toy shark deflated with a sad sighing sound.

'I think that's significant,' grinned Cavan. 'Or it will be, when I've worked it out.'

'I'm pretending it's you and I've punctured your ego,' she explained drily.

He winced and left with a cheerful whistle piercing the air. He thumped down the stairs two at a time. Bethany ran into the bathroom, dragging off her nightie and clambering into her underwear, a pair of jeans and a cotton shirt. Inside two minutes she was dashing into the kitchen, her cap of dark, glossy hair bouncing, her face bright pink from a quick dousing with ice-cold water.

'What kept you?' he asked laconically, picking up his fork. She ignored him and tucked into her breakfast. 'You have one hell of an appetite,' he remarked softly. 'It matches mine. Sorry! Pax!' he cried, holding up his hands in apology at her fierce glare. 'It's habit, I'm afraid. Put me in front of a beautiful woman——'

'You can cut out the flattery. I'm in my scruff, without make-up, and I probably have egg on my chin,' she said in a matter-of-fact tone.

'You have,' he sighed, reaching forwards with his forefinger and gently dabbing at the corner of her mouth. The gesture was unnervingly sensual. 'Somehow the egg decoration makes no difference. You're a *woman*.' She gave him her most withering look, offended by being lumped in with the mass-market appeal. 'The lines on your forehead have gone,' he observed.

'What?' She forked up a piece of bacon and held her fork suspended in mid-air while she tried to work out what he was getting at.

'You've relaxed,' he murmured.

'That sounds rather unwise,' she said drily. 'If I had any sense, I'd still have all the barricades up.'

His mouth quirked appealingly at one corner, but his eyes were thoughtful. 'The war should never have started. It certainly shouldn't continue. I was worried about you, Beth. You were so uptight when you arrived here a few days ago——'

'It was hardly surprising,' she said, munching on a piece of crisp bacon. He'd cooked it to perfection, just how she liked it. Perhaps he'd remembered. 'I'd left the village in a cloud of exhaust fumes and a state of hysterics,' she added, trying to make light of it all. 'I never thought I could look the butcher in the face again after you'd bent me back in that ridiculous Hollywood pose and kissed me outside his shop.'

Cavan didn't smile at her deliberately flippant description of their stormy parting. 'I was trying to make you see sense,' he said in a low voice.

'Sense?' she frowned. 'That's hardly fair—you're the one who'd lost his senses. Surely it wasn't stupid of me to say I wanted to buy you out. I wanted to buy the hotel from you, to make it mine and Mawgan's again, and you refused——'

'I told you,' he said shortly, 'I didn't want your money.'

'Dan's money,' she corrected.

'All right,' he muttered. 'Have it your own way. However, if you'd asked me to *give* Portallen to you because you were homeless and it had once belonged to your father, I would have done. But no, you had to insult me by flashing around the money you'd acquired because your husband had a fatal accident at work,' he growled.

She flinched at his cruel bluntness. 'You wouldn't have given me Portallen,' she said, tipping up her chin defensively. 'You never give anything away free!'

'Once I did, more's the pity. Something very precious to me,' he said quietly. 'But you never knew about that and never will. Bethany, I did feel sorry for you and the way the villagers had treated you. I would have let you have the Inn. But you would have had to beg me first. That's what I wanted from you—some acknowledgement that——'

'Oh, Cavan! Your obsession with dominating me is never far from the surface, is it?' she broke in sadly. She paused and plunged on, 'You'd even go so far as to arrange a hate campaign to drive me into your clutches.'

Cavan stiffened, his eyes a fierce blue in his tanned face. 'Me? Arrange... Is that what you believe?' he asked softly, his body totally still.

Her hands trembled but she persevered. She had to say it. 'I've thought about it for a long time. There was no one else with the motivation or the devious kind of mind to want to do such a thing. You wrote those poison-pen letters.'

She bit her lip at the unnerving way his jaw clenched and her eyes were drawn to his fork, quivering in mid-air, shaking with pure rage in his bone-crushing fist.

When he spoke, however, it was in a tightly controlled voice with no emotion in it whatever. 'I never thought you mistrusted and hated me to that extent,' he said in a harsh whisper.

'I've always mistrusted you,' she retorted shakily.

'And you think I wrote the letters.'

'Yes, I do,' she whispered.

His inscrutable eyes examined hers. 'I'm the worst person you can think of.' She was silent. 'Mawgan was wrong, then. He said we'd get on together.'

'He was wrong,' she agreed, keeping her voice even.

He put down his fork very carefully and leaned back in his chair. 'I tell you this, Bethany,' he said in a tone utterly devoid of all expression, 'I did not have anything at all to do with those letters, or with the gossip. I swear that on my mother's grave. You can believe me or not, as you choose, but that's the truth.'

He meant that. No one could doubt the honesty in his eyes. Bethany bit her lip. 'I—I was wrong. I was sure... I—I'm sorry,' she said, distressed by the hard glitter in his eyes. 'You're rightly angry with me,' she added, hanging her head guiltily. 'I just couldn't think of anyone else who wanted to see me wriggle, who resented the easy way I'd acquired a lot of money. You had to work so hard——'

'So you fled to Bodmin.' He seemed to have dismissed the matter because he continued eating as if he didn't care what she said. 'Have you been happy there?'

She hesitated. There was nothing to be gained in lying. 'No. I'm only happy here,' she answered honestly.

'Then why stay somewhere you hate? You could go anywhere in the world.'

'I wanted to be near enough to Mawgan so he could visit me. I couldn't live here because of the hostility and because I wouldn't have been able to avoid you.'

He was lifting his cup when she said that, and Bethany saw that it didn't shake even a fraction. So he'd known that she had hated him enough to deny herself her own home, her own brother. Ached for him, hated him, they were the same violent feelings, which she longed to discard for a more normal relationship with a less unpredictable man. But she was bound hand and foot, body and soul to Cavan. For her own sanity she had to keep clear of him.

'Go on.'

'I wish you'd go back to London,' she said woodenly. 'It would make my life easier. I'm sure I could gradually persuade the villagers that I'm not a selfish jet-setter. It would be possible for me to live here, then. Where I belong.'

'Your life would be easier,' he agreed non-committally, 'but less interesting. Tell me honestly. Did you love Dan, really love him?' he asked suddenly, startling her.

'I told you,' she said stiffly. 'That's off limits.'

'You've answered,' he said enigmatically.

'No, I haven't! Oh, darn you! I don't know why you keep making me lose my temper! Let's keep our relationship to a polite working one, shall we?'

'If that's what you want,' he said, his eyes watching her over the rim of his cup.

'I don't want any other kind.'

'So you keep on telling me,' he murmured softly. Then he seemed to abandon the conversation, and pushed his chair back. 'Very well. We'll try. I'm going to a farm sale this morning. Want to come? You might see some useful items for the Inn. You can tie a rope around my hands if you like.'

She smiled. 'Once I might have said that I'd rather it was your neck,' she said wryly, risking a joke at her own expense. Cavan's eyes smiled back at hers. 'OK,' she agreed. 'We might as well make a start.'

'That's what I was thinking.'

Bethany frowned at Cavan, but he looked perfectly innocent. As she helped him put away the breakfast things and stack the dishwasher, it occurred to her that he'd never been innocent in his life. Her body tensed and her mind sharpened in preparation for the next few hours. He'd called a truce, but she couldn't trust him.

Disconcertingly, she noticed that adrenalin was making her feel full of energy and rather exhilarated, as if something in her found it exciting that she and Cavan were working together. Even more alarming was the fact that he, too, was fired with exuberance. Her awareness of him was intensified, and she saw that his face was alive with a vital energy, his whole body taut and poised like a high-tension wire.

And in that state he was dangerously attractive.

They borrowed a Land Rover and drove up the river valley through unspoilt woodland. Cavan didn't spoil her pleasure by teasing her or making sarcastic remarks.

They talked about Mawgan, and Bethany relaxed completely, thrilled that her brother would have the opportunity to realise his considerable potential at last.

'We'll split forces,' Cavan said when they arrived at the farm. 'Meet you by the hot-dog stand in half an hour. That'll give us time to compare notes.'

Bethany was a little disappointed. She'd looked forward to walking around with him. When they came nearer to the cluster of buildings she realised how run-down the farm had become. 'It's an "All Up" auction by the looks of it,' she said, not liking what she saw.

''Fraid so. He must be deeply in debt for all these personal items to be included in the sale,' commented Cavan. 'See you in a while.' He strode off across the farmyard, looking surprisingly at home among the deer-stalker hats, the home-knitted jumpers and the rash of Barbour jackets.

She was back by the hot-dog van in twenty minutes, deeply distressed. She'd met the farmer's wife, who had been white-faced and upset from watching strangers foraging through her possessions.

'Cavan!' she yelled, when she saw his dark head above the jostling people near the tool shed. She hurried over, anxious to leave.

'Beth? You've been quick. I haven't finished yet.'

His familiar face and body looked immensely comforting to her eyes. Her impulse to throw herself in his arms appalled her. She was upset, but that was no reason for her to look to him for consolation.

'I didn't see anything we could use. It was a waste of time,' she told him tersely.

'Just come on a final tour around with me and then we'll go,' he said, tucking her arm in his. 'They're about to start on selling the first lot in a few minutes.'

With extreme reluctance, she let herself be dragged around the sheds and stores packed with boxes of crockery, lampshades, farm equipment, garden tools... Bethany watched the sharp-eyed dealers and avaricious-looking women picking over what represented a few generations of a farming family's life. Miserably she wondered if this was what had happened when she had let an agent sell all of Dan's things and hers—everything they'd shared together.

'I want to go now,' she mumbled.

Cavan turned her around to face him. 'Look at me, Bethany,' he said in a low tone. She flicked sullen eyes up at him and then lowered her lids to hide the feelings which were churning away inside her. 'You look dreadful. Is something the matter? Tell me!' he ordered.

She could tell from the way he spoke and the way he'd planted his legs apart—in fact, the whole set of his body—that he wouldn't rest till she'd answered. 'It's awful. It's like vultures picking over a carcass,' she said with a small shudder as she looked around.

She heard the auctioneer's voice in the dilapidated barn ringing out. 'Two-pound bid? Don't do anythin' rash, me dears.'

'This is one of the harsh realities of life,' said Cavan quietly.

'Yes, but,' she explained huskily, 'it seems incredibly sad. The farm here has died on its feet and the farmer is selling everything he ever owned. Did you see his wife? She shouldn't be here. She shouldn't be watching people poking around her things.'

'I know. I used the auctioneer's car-phone to order a taxi for her, and shoved her into it,' said Cavan. 'I felt terribly sorry for her. It's an awful situation.'

'That was nice of you,' said Bethany impulsively.

Her hand was caught by his. 'That's the first time you've ever said anything remotely pleasant to me,' Cavan told her in astonishment. 'I hope it won't be the last.'

'Lot two. Come on, now, pound to start, pound to start...'

Bethany tore her eyes away from his, confused. 'That bid is for the box of wellington boots,' she said hurriedly. She caught sight of a woman laughing at the farmer's taste in paperbacks, and bristled. 'Look, Cavan!' she cried indignantly. 'The nerve of it!'

'I agree,' he said, his brows drawn together heavily. 'I must say,' he mused, reaching to test the weight of a log-splitter, 'if I owned these tools I wouldn't want to sell them. There's a lifetime's collection here. Must have been his pride and joy.'

'You do understand, then,' she said, surprised at his sensitivity. 'Let's go. I can't stand it, Cavan. It makes me feel sick. It's like invading his privacy. Take me away.'

Her sad eyes lifted to his warily. There was a guarded expression on his face.

'Fifty pence a door ain't bad, me 'andsome...'

Bethany was agonising over her misdirected emotions. Her distress was magnified because she felt more sorrow for the farmer and his family than she had at selling her things in Aberdeen. Maybe she'd been in shock. Or perhaps it was because it was a part of her life that had never touched her emotions at all.

'It can't be easy, losing your family home,' Cavan said.

She started, her mind switching immediately to the prospect of losing Portallen. 'I couldn't bear this to happen to my home, to the Inn, Cavan,' she admitted huskily.

'I realise that. I once thought you didn't care about it, but now I know different. Look, Beth, this sale has upset you and I wish it hadn't. But perhaps it's no bad thing. Fix this in your mind; remember it all. Because there are going to be times in the next few months when you will want to go back on our arrangement and when your instincts will tell you to run away again—and that you must never do.'

His hands slid to her shoulders and he forced her to keep looking at him when she tried to avoid his glittering eyes.

'Why do you think that I'll want to leave?' she asked, her voice cracking. 'What—what are you planning for me?'

'I'm looking ahead, knowing how we behave together. We're going to argue and make up, we'll want to throttle each other and we'll also desperately want to make love——'

'*No!*' she ground out in quick denial.

'I'm being honest, Bethany. I'm preparing you,' he said ruthlessly. 'Be absolutely clear on this; if you haven't the guts to carry out the renovation of the Portallen Inn, I will put it on the market faster than you can hurl insults at me, because I'll have no reason to keep it or the memories it has for me.'

'You hate it?' she asked, wide-eyed.

'You'll find out what I feel over the next few months, I hope,' he said, his mouth crooking wryly at one corner. 'What happens to the hotel is up to you. Until now, whether you've lived there or not, you've always known it's been there, with a room for you if you've wanted. With Mawgan out of the way——'

'You planned that?' she breathed.

'Every step of the way,' he agreed, his eyes remorseless. 'I wanted this arrangement to be between us and no one else.'

'That sounds like revenge,' she said huskily.

'Does it? It's not meant to. I wanted the coast clear so we could have a free run of the house. I don't want anything to interfere with my intention to make you work for me.' He paused. 'This sale has brought the situation sharply into focus. Portallen represents your childhood memories. I *own* those memories, Bethany, more than you realise. Go back on our deal, and, as God is my witness, I'll sell everything: your mother's curtains, the linen, the tablecloths she embroidered, the lampshades she made. Your father's home-made shelves and the books he left to me, the Toby Jugs he collected——'

'Stop!' she whispered, her face as white as a sheet. Tears filled her eyes. 'Oh, Cavan, for God's sake, stop!' A tear ran down her cheek. She sped across the cracked concrete yard to the field where the cars were parked, and waited blindly by the Land Rover.

The hotel was full of memories. Dim ones of her mother, happy, loving ones of her father and Mawgan. Turbulent ones of Cavan, thundering through the house like a line-squall. Her eyes closed. Finding him asleep one morning, after he'd stayed out all night, his lashes thick and appealing on his sleep-warm cheeks. Seeing him sitting in the kitchen mending a cormorant's broken wing, his forehead creased in concentration. His voice, his vitality, his hunger for life.

All that she'd lose if he carried out his threat.

Cavan came up after a while and helped her in, then drove off without a word, tension in every line of his body.

She didn't care. The way she felt, she never wanted to speak to him again. Hurting her was becoming a way of life to him. He was incredibly cruel. She stiffened as Cavan applied the brakes and drew the Land Rover to a halt near the desolate, ivy-clad ruins of an old engine-house where copper had once been mined.

'Calmer now? We have to talk,' he said expressionlessly.

She slid a quick glance to his hard profile. He was going to lecture her. 'No,' was all she could manage.

Cavan let out a sigh of exasperation. 'I can't stand this, Bethany,' he muttered.

'Then release me!' she cried passionately.

He flinched. 'I can't.'

'Why? You don't even like me! Do we have to have this cat and mouse game just to satisfy your vanity? Do you have to keep blackmailing me?' she continued wildly.

'I didn't know you'd be so affected by the farm sale,' he grated.

She grew wary, knowing she dared not tell him the whole truth. 'Perhaps I should tell you just where your blundering schemes have taken you. The auction upset me because I'd sold all of Dan's things in the same way,' she cried unhappily, wanting to hurt him as he'd hurt her. 'Every single thing in the house. Our furniture, our bed and bedding——' Cavan winced and she gritted her teeth and carried on '—his clothes, his effects, the records we'd played together——'

'All right, Bethany! Please; this is not helping either of us!' he cried, his face haggard. 'You don't need to go on. Oh, God!' he groaned. 'I had no idea, I didn't know——'

'No. You were too hell-bent on making your damn point, weren't you?' she said bitterly. He was silent, every muscle in his body flexed and tense. 'You bastard. And you wonder why I don't trust you, why I regard you with contempt. Take me home,' she finished wearily.

'Bodmin?' he asked hoarsely.

'Portallen.' She noticed that he didn't make any sarcastic remark about it not really being her home.

'I'm sorry. I'm truly sorry. I ask you to forgive me for being so crass and blundering in on your feelings.'

She was startled. He'd never apologised so humbly in the whole of his life, and it sounded as if the apology had been wrenched out of him. 'The damage has been done,' she said flatly, and suddenly she felt her eyes fill with tears.

'Yes, and I wish it hadn't.' He turned in the seat to face her. 'Oh, Beth,' he said gently. 'Please don't cry.'

The tears ran down her cheeks. 'I'm so tired of struggling to keep my neck above water,' she sobbed. 'If only things would go smoothly for once——'

'They will,' he promised, dabbing at her eyes tenderly with his handkerchief. 'Poor Beth. No one's ever looked after you, have they? You were so young when your mother died and you took charge of your brother. Always the tower of strength, hiding your own needs. You wouldn't even ask Rosie for advice, would you?'

'I did once,' she muttered, flushing a little. 'She told me to go and get what I wanted.'

He roared with laughter. 'Sounds like Ma,' he chuckled. 'Nothing subtle about her, was there?' he added fondly. 'Bright red hair, eyelashes you could fan your face with and a heart as big as the Albert Hall. I wept when she died, Beth,' he said huskily.

Her eyes widened. 'Oh, Cavan!' she exclaimed unhappily, seeing his bleak face. A few more tears fell for him. 'I'm so sorry. I was in Mexico when I heard.' She reached out a friendly hand to his.

He gave her a gentle smile. 'We had one hell of a Wake. Went on for days. I miss her very much. Do you know, she'd given me the same advice that she gave to you? That's why I had left Portallen in the first place, knowing I'd never make my fortune there. I gave myself five years to get what I wanted, but...' he shrugged and looked away '... I got the timing wrong,' he breathed. 'For the first time in my life, I was too late.'

'At twenty-two?' she asked in surprise. 'Cavan, you were doing well then. And it wasn't long before you made your first million. We were all very proud.'

'You never said,' he pointed out. 'You kept your feelings and your thoughts to yourself. Beth, I think it's time you shared your problems with someone and leaned on a strong shoulder.'

It sounded wonderful. He was right; she'd never been free of responsibility, had never fooled around like the other kids, but had snatched brief moments of leisure and made hurried visits to the beach in the hope that Cavan would admire her.

'I'm just over-sensitive at the moment,' she confessed, sniffing. 'Coming back and finding the villagers still unfriendly was a bit of a shock. Mawgan said the trouble had blown over.'

'I can help there. Let me ease that particular situation,' he suggested. 'And please, turn to me for help. You have never let me help you before, but I'm asking you to stop trying to deal with all your difficulties on your own. My shoulders are broad; lean on them. Why be so prickly where I'm concerned? Give me the benefit of the doubt for a change.'

She could hardly tell him that she erected unnecessary barriers to stop herself from leaping over them and throwing herself into his arms. 'Don't tease me,' she said miserably.

'Beth.' He put a brotherly arm around her shoulder and took over the business of drying her tears. 'I'll be gentle with you if you'll be gentle with me.'

She managed a small smile. Her eyes slanted up to his and met only openness. 'I suppose we ought to be friends,' she said. 'Break the habit of a lifetime...'

He laughed and gave her a squeeze. 'We'll put up a united front and then the villagers will be totally disarmed,' he said comfortingly. 'Once they're eating out of your hands, you'll find life a hell of a lot easier.'

He dropped a kiss on her nose and then, after a brief pause when she sat without moving, he kissed her lips gently. For a fleeting second, Bethany thought the kiss was deepening, but to her mingled disappointment and relief he drew away and started up the Land Rover. It was hard when he was foul to her. It was worse when he was nice.

Far from being settled, her emotions were turbulent as a stormy sea. Staring out at the tumbled stones of the giant engine-house and its tall chimney smothered in choking ivy, she mused that her life seemed to be desolate and in empty, silent ruins, too, with no future. Cavan had shown her a glimpse of a tender, caring man. That had made her own feelings for him more powerful. And she was unhappier than ever. She had neither the home nor the man she wanted.

CHAPTER FIVE

THEY drove through the village, and Cavan stopped by the butcher's shop, saying he had an order to collect. Knowing he had to return the Land Rover, Bethany said she'd walk back to the hotel. At the bottom of the street was a group of fishermen, their dark Celtic faces watching her sullenly. Her steps faltered but she kept going.

'Mornin', Beth. Not married Cavan yet, then?'

She came to a halt a few feet from them, disconcerted by the spiteful tone of Rowan's voice. Married? she thought, a pang piercing her heart. 'I'm not looking for self-torture, Rowan,' she said in a low tone.

The men laughed in delight. 'Still fightin', then?' asked Rowan. 'And come back for more! What about they kisses, eh?'

She blushed, knowing he referred to the day of her departure. The violent, intensely sexual kiss was engraved on her memory and was uncomfortably unforgettable.

'I've returned to do something for Mawgan,' she said with quiet dignity.

Every man there scowled at her. 'Arr. We was saying; Beth could do somethin' fer the village,' growled Ewen. 'All they millions of pounds wasted on a woman's back. New storm-gate's needed, you know.'

She looked at them in dismay. 'I—I can't——'

'Can't? Won't, more like it,' accused Rowan roughly.

'You'll get your gate, Ewen,' said Cavan's firm voice behind her.

Like the men, Bethany heard the slicing steel in his words. They tipped their caps respectfully, and she felt her body relax with relief. Her legs were trembling. Ewen sniffed again. 'Could get it quicker if Beth weren't so selfish 'n mean——'

She drew in her breath sharply, and Cavan's hand descended heavily on Ewen's shoulder. Bethany couldn't make out whether it was a friendly gesture or one of warning. 'Bethany's trying to sort out her life,' explained Cavan in a confidential voice. 'She needs us. Don't you, darling?'

Bethany's eyes widened at the deeply affectionate way he said that. Before she could gather her wits and deny that there was any affection between them, Ewen eyed her speculatively.

'So you did come back fer more!' he said in his lilting Cornish brogue, as she dazedly shook his hand. 'You two always was larkin' around. She your'n, boy?'

Cavan looked bashful. 'Come on, now,' he grinned, shifting his feet. 'Give a guy a break.'

Bethany was open-mouthed at his deceit. And his skill. Ewen was briefly disarmed, a faint smile appearing on his face. Then it vanished. 'Village don't like her,' he said flatly.

'Isn't my judgement good enough for you?' asked Cavan quietly. The men shifted awkwardly. 'Come on, man, the past is past. We've all matured since that tittle-tattle. Beth is working for me. She's helping Mawgan and me to undo the damage that cowboy firm did. You're always mizzening in your beer mug that it was about time Portallen got its character back, aren't you?'

Bethany saw that the men were laughing with Cavan at the discomfited Ewen, and that Cavan had enough goodwill to get away with the gentle ribbing.

'I'll give you mizzen,' chuckled Ewen. 'You'll be miz-
zenin' when I've beaten you at darts!'

'Best of nine,' challenged Cavan, his eyes dancing.
'Oh, before we go,' he added, 'I'm relying on you all to
help Bethany for me if she has any serious problems.
I'll be glad of your support. I don't want any hold-ups.
You know how impatient I am,' he grinned.

'Womenfolk tells us so,' chuckled Rowan. 'Mebbe us'd
help.'

'Thanks,' smiled Cavan. 'She might need it. You can
see how things are. She's a little dazed. I've rather swept
her off her feet.' He glanced with fond concern at her
stunned face.

Bethany found her voice. 'I don't——'

'It's OK, darling. They know me. They understand.'
Cavan curved a possessive arm around her shoulder.

'No, it's——'

'Hush.' Her voice was muffled by Cavan's mouth. She
heard the men chuckling, and Cavan began to kiss her
more thoroughly, his arms imprisoning her. When the
men's footsteps had died away, he released her. 'You
must go with the tide, not against it,' he said softly.
'Couldn't you see that the men would begin to accept
you if they thought you and I were friends?'

'Friends, maybe. That's ludicrous enough, but do we
have to act like lovers too?' she asked huskily, her mouth
burning and hungry.

'It's what they've expected since we first collided,' he
smiled.

Bethany found it hard to tear her eyes away from his
tempting mouth, and that irritated her beyond belief.
One kiss and she was his. She wanted to grind her teeth
in rage. 'I can't think why!' she snapped. 'That's the
most illogical statement you've ever made!'

He heaved a great sigh. 'I could see how upset you were,' he explained. 'I was thinking on my feet and trying to get you out of a tight spot. They still resent your money. Bethany, I know you don't like this but it's a temporary solution. It won't hurt you to be linked with me. They've been nudging and winking about your rescue and how you've come to live in the hotel. Word will get around that you and I are an "item", and the village will gradually accept you to their bosom——'

'Because I'm your girlfriend?' she asked in astonishment. 'What have you done? Brainwashed them all? I know you'd never be able to buy them outright.'

'They've discovered a few of my better qualities,' he said laconically. 'I haven't been around much but we've learnt a lot about each other over the last six or seven years. Look, Bethany, I'm doing this for another reason. If you're working here for the next few months and you need help when I'm not around, then where will you turn?'

'I hadn't thought. The workmen on the hotel?' she suggested.

'Supposing you need help outside working hours? No. You must be able to call on the villagers. You of all people know how everyone pulls together in a crisis. You could have trouble one day, whether it's a burst watermain or a storm, or a fire...' His dark eyes brooded on her. 'If I'm on the other side of the world, I want to know that——' His voice stopped short. 'That the Inn won't be destroyed because no one will come to your aid,' he finished curtly.

'Protecting your interests,' she said cynically.

'Yes.' His eyes gleamed and he seemed amused for a moment. 'There could hardly be any other reason, could there?'

Bethany frowned, picturing the scene he'd painted. 'You're right,' she acknowledged with reluctance. 'I don't want anything to happen to Portallen either. But I'd rather it was because I was accepted for myself, rather than as your appendage!'

He smiled apologetically. 'You can clear things up later. Give them time to get used to you first. Sorry about the kiss. I had to shut you up somehow. It seemed better than gagging you with my hand. That *would* have been suspicious.'

'I suppose so,' she muttered. 'But I wish you weren't so free with your lips. They seem to be glued to mine at the slightest opportunity.'

Cavan's hand curved around the back of her neck. 'Well, that's your fault for having such infinitely kissable lips,' he said lightly.

'Try exercising a little self-control,' she retorted waspishly.

Back home in the kitchen, Bethany made herself a sandwich while Cavan watched, his hands thrust deep into his pockets. 'I think, since there's a deadline looming, we might as well start discussing the renovation,' he said casually.

'I'd like that,' she replied with enthusiasm. It would mean that his mind—and possibly his hands and mouth—would be occupied.

They argued, of course, but productively. Bethany was a little disconcerted to discover how much she was privately enjoying the cut and thrust of the session. Cavan was a quick thinker, picking up the threads of her suggestions fast, and when she struggled to describe an effect she was aiming for he skilfully drew enough information from her to clarify the idea and commit it to paper.

Bethany's excitement increased. If she could carry out everything they had discussed, Portallen would look wonderful, and she couldn't wait to start. Cavan didn't think small.

Her eyes glowed as she looked at Cavan, arguing about the placing of a fire escape so that it would be unobtrusive. His body seemed fired with energy as he leaned across the table, his big hands gesticulating and his face... Her heart lurched crazily.

Dynamic, compelling, he was irresistible. That expressive curve of his mouth, the gleaming white teeth as he made a joke, the softening of his eloquent eyes as she laughed; all these added up to a man so vitally alive that his life-force was almost tangible. And whose sexual chemistry electrified her.

'I'm hungry,' she said suddenly, breaking into his persuasive argument.

'Me too.' He made no effort to rise, but sat very still, and the long, slow look which passed between them created an unbearable tension.

'I'll put something in the microwave,' she said, getting up blindly and grabbing the first thing she could find in the freezer.

'My goodness, you are woolly-minded. If you don't mind,' said Cavan softly, taking the packet from her hand, 'I'll give the spinach a miss. It might suit Popeye but I like variety. Could I have one of those pasta dishes instead?'

She flushed and fumbled in the freezer for something more suitable. Fortunately he was still so intent on discussing the renovation that he forgot to tease her about her confusion—or perhaps he hadn't realised what had caused it. In any case, she was more than glad to continue talking over supper.

After eating, by mutual consent they pushed the dishes to one side and carried on.

'I thought, now we've solved most of the major problems of alteration and the re-arrangement of rooms, that we'd have a brain-storming session,' Cavan suggested. 'How about listing everything we can think of that a luxury hotel should have?'

'Keeping it in the country-house style,' she reminded him. She was pleased about that. It would seem almost as if the Portallen Inn was her home.

'Sure. Let's take it as read that we'd have antique furniture, good furnishings and china. What small touches do we add?'

'Oyster satin sheets?' she asked innocently.

He grinned and wagged his finger at her. 'I'll never live that down, will I? Who let out my guilty secret?'

'The hotel receptionist,' she said cynically. 'The one you brought down to stay.'

'Oh, yes. I didn't know you two had chatted. She was incredibly jealous of you.'

'Me? I was eighteen! She was mature, smart, worldly wise and very beautiful.'

'And very perceptive,' he added enigmatically. 'Let's get on with the luxury items—oyster satin sheets being taken for granted,' he said with a wicked look at her.

'A library of local books and information,' she offered enthusiastically. 'And a range of glossy magazines,' she added wistfully. It had been years since she'd been able to buy any.

'Padded hangers,' he added, writing the ideas down. 'Women like those. Hairdriers. Shoe-cleaning service.'

'Plants. Palm trees. Blue or green striped awnings.'

'Home-grown food, discreet service, two large basins in each en suite bathroom, big vanity units with those enormous, well-lit mirrors——'

She nodded approvingly. Just what she'd like. He certainly had the finger on female pulses, she thought wryly. 'It must look cosy and welcoming. I wish we had a fire in the hall. How about a grand piano, country flowers freshly picked from the garden, lots of rugs——?'

Cavan reached out his hand to cover hers. 'Hold on a moment.' He scribbled furiously and then removed his hand when he'd caught up with their ideas. 'And a conservatory where we—they—could eat breakfast, pure linen on the beds—oh, and women love having dozens of fluffy towels around.'

Bethany made no comment, though his intimate knowledge of women's likes was beginning to irk her. 'This is going to cost a fortune. You haven't once said you can't afford any of this. Will it ever pay?' She looked up, and thought he'd been smirking at her remark, but he met her eyes quite calmly.

'It'll be worth every penny,' he said blandly. 'How about fast-filling baths for the man in a hurry?'

'Deep ones, cast iron,' she said dreamily, 'each one provided with a yellow plastic duck.'

Cavan laughed. 'Whatever you say,' he grinned. 'If you like it, we'll have it. Tomorrow I'm going to get some plans drawn up by an architect. In the meantime you can start searching for colour schemes on the themes you suggested earlier. I want to see all the material and wallpaper you choose, remember. OK. That's enough for now,' he said, shutting his folder.

'Oh!' she cried, disappointed.

'Enjoyed it?' he queried softly.

'Enormously. I always enjoy my work,' she answered quickly, hoping he hadn't got the wrong idea. But it would have taken a fool not to notice how well they'd sparked ideas off each other, and Cavan was no fool.

'But this is for your old home; you must feel differently about it,' he probed.

'Since the circumstances are that I can't properly live here, then doing it up sympathetically—and having a hand in the conversion—is at least a second best,' she answered stiffly.

'You could live here permanently if you wanted to,' murmured Cavan, a strange light glittering in his eyes. 'With no ties unless you want them,' he said in his gravelly voice.

Pain etched lines on her face. Something in his tone told her that there would be ties, enough to rope her down so that she was totally under his control. Oh, yes, she thought, she wanted so badly to live in the new, restored hotel.

Unintentionally, she and Cavan had been planning her dream home.

'That's not fair,' she said shakily. 'You're only saying that to raise my hopes, and then you'll announce some kind of condition or say that you're going to live here yourself.'

The skin on his face seemed taut. 'If I did say I intended to live here——'

'Oh, you wouldn't!' she cried in disappointment. 'There's only one staff bedroom. You said I'd own half of the hotel, and I thought that bedroom was for me or Mawgan.' She groaned. 'God, you're cruel! You've got me hooked and you're constantly letting out the line and reeling it in, aren't you? You show me how lovely it will be here and torment me by putting it in my mind that I could make it my home.'

'You'd like that?' he asked softly.

Her mouth twisted bitterly. 'Of course I'd like that! What are you trying to do to me? Rip your damn hook through my body? If you're intending to live here...'

She flicked up her eyes at him and gave him a shrewd look. 'You're not suggesting we share the same bedroom?' she asked tightly.

'It's a single,' he pointed out. 'It would be a bit cramped.'

She let out an annoyed breath. 'Everything was going so well, and you've ruined it with your innuendo. Yes, I know we have to work together tomorrow. That's why I'm not throwing things at you,' she said irritably. 'I need a breath of fresh air. Excuse me.' When she got to her feet, she realised how stiff she was from sitting for so long. 'I'm going for a walk.'

'It's dark.'

'There's a hunter's moon. Anyway, I know this area blindfold.'

'Nevertheless,' he said quietly, reaching out to help her into her jacket, 'I'm coming.'

She shrugged. 'Short of murder, which has occasionally crossed my mind, I can't stop you,' she conceded with studied indifference.

Striding unhappily ahead of him, she heard him collect something from his car and then hurry up the cliff path after her. When she reached the top of the cliff, she looked down on the white surf crashing on the black rocks, and lifted her face to the cool night breeze. Her head tipped back to gaze at the stars in the intense black sky, each tiny twinkling light patterning the sky like silver glitter.

And her love for Portallen and for Cavan mingled, her desolation at having neither of them making her want to open her mouth and rage at the fates. To live in Portallen with him. That would be her eternal fantasy. She stopped dead. She loved Cavan. Her hand shook as it went to her brow. She loved him—desperately, deeply. It was no longer an obsession, a kind of angry reaction, or even some carnal need. She wanted to spend the rest of her life with him, to seek out all that was tender and loving within him, to share...

'Hold this a minute, will you?' muttered Cavan, sounding preoccupied.

'Mmm?' She looked down in surprise at the wooden reel he'd thrust into her hand. 'What on earth are you doing?' she cried, seeing that he was solemnly unravelling a long-tailed kite.

'I'm unravelling a long-tailed kite,' he said.

'It's dark!' she protested with a half-laugh.

'There's a hunter's moon and the kite knows this place blindfold,' he said drily. 'Right. Let the string out a bit so I can go ahead.'

'I don't believe I'm doing this!' muttered Bethany. 'Flying a kite in the middle of the night!'

'Let it go a little,' called Cavan, ignoring her and intent on the matter in hand.

She could see his big familiar face and his hands holding up the bright yellow kite. Her hands felt the tug as the wind jiggled impatiently at the kite, eager to take it and drag it away. Cautiously she let out the line, and the kite soared into the sky.

'More!' urged Cavan, hurrying up to her, his eyes on the kite. But there was something strange in his voice, a fierce urgency and an undercurrent of excitement, and her heart opened to him, the joy filling her body.

The kite was fighting to be free, the strength of the wind surprising. She could feel the small gusts which grabbed the kite greedily and, needing some outlet for her soaring emotions, she began to run the line out faster till it was at full stretch, taut, fiercely dragging at her hands.

'I can't hold it!' she cried in excitement.

Cavan's hands clamped over hers. He stood behind her, shielding her body from the wind, tucking her into him and letting her feel the struggle between kite and wind. It was almost as powerful as the one going on inside her. She leaned into him a little and his arms tightened imperceptibly, and she was happy.

Bethany felt like a child again. She laughed at the way the wind sought to take the kite from them, a surge of triumph going through her as they succeeded in harnessing its power. Their faces were upturned to that small yellow shape high in the sky with its fluttering tail, glorying in the force which they were battling with, the fierce, relentless force of nature.

And Cavan showed her how to make the kite dip and swoop, to dance in the sky as if it were alive. They were both laughing, the wind catching her throat and filling her body with a sparkle as potent as champagne.

'Let's run,' suggested Cavan, elation lighting his face.

Without waiting for her agreement, he grabbed her hand and pulled her along. Knowing the smooth lie of the grass, she ran fearlessly, barely managing to keep up with him. Now and again they looked back together to see the kite obediently rushing through the air behind them. Almost at the edge of the grass, just before the sheep fence, they came to a halt, panting and laughing.

Bethany was crushed in Cavan's arms, her head roughly tipped back, and then she felt the warmth of Cavan's face against her cheek as he hugged her. She pushed against his body, but there wasn't an inch of movement.

'Cavan——'

The wonderful softness of his lips met hers in a long, endless kiss, and she was so exhilarated and happy that she sank into his arms more deeply, feeling liberated and free up there on the cliff, with the kite hovering above them.

It was almost as if they were on another planet, she thought dazedly, as his kiss grew more insistent.

'God! I could stand here all night,' he whispered. His mouth passionately devoured her face, her throat, her neck, filling her with the changing sensations as she felt his lips, moist tongue and gently savaging teeth roaming over her skin.

'This has gone far enough. I don't think we ought——' Bethany gasped and let out a small moan. 'Please don't,' she whispered in alarm, as Cavan's hand slid under her shirt. But she leaned into him, shuddering at the touch of his fingers, which were sliding inexorably up each rib. And then they stopped. Her eyes flicked open to plead with his, though she didn't know if she was begging him to stop or demanding that he should reach out and touch her throbbing breast.

'You are so beautiful,' he murmured softly. 'More beautiful and desirable than any woman I've ever known—or ever will know.'

Bethany swallowed. 'I—I——' she croaked. In dismay, she moistened her lips.

With a sexy growl, Cavan dipped his head and took her tongue between his lips, drawing it into his mouth. It was such an erotic sensation that Bethany's whole body weakened, and she would have slid to the ground if he hadn't supported her. Gently he took the kite from her trembling hand and tucked it securely in his belt, his eyes never leaving hers for a second, holding her a willing prisoner.

She lifted her arms and brought them around his neck, arching her back so that they were body to body, thigh to thigh. Hardly knowing what she was doing, she drew his dark head down to her waiting mouth and kissed him sweetly on the lips, then let her hot, urgent mouth explore his face.

'Go on, go on,' he urged huskily, his hands caressing her back. Then they were smoothing over her buttocks in a rhythmic movement that was driving her crazy.

It was as if she was drunk on the magic of the night, intoxicated by the taste, the smell, the sound of Cavan and Portallen. Without a thought for the consequences, she abandoned herself to his arms, his lips, his seductive voice and exciting touch, letting him push off her jacket and impatiently fumbling with the zip on his till he pushed her hands away and removed it himself, his hands shaking as much as hers had.

They were a few inches apart, staring at one another, panting slightly, and Bethany wanted him with a pain that was tearing her apart, filling her body with a thudding, pounding heat.

'I'm setting the kite free,' said Cavan softly, releasing the reel from his belt and holding it in his hand.

Bethany's eyes widened. 'Why?' she whispered.

'It's begging to be free,' he said huskily, his gaze dark and savage with passion. 'It can't tell me in words but I know from its every movement that it wants to soar as far as it can go. It's been controlled for too long.'

Her breath caught in her throat as he opened his hand and for a few seconds the reel remained almost motionless as if it didn't know it was free. Then the wind tugged at the kite and she looked up as it was jerked away from Cavan's hand. For a moment the kite lurched in all directions and then it began to rise, higher and higher, up to the stars.

And then she couldn't see it any more.

She was trembling. Cavan reached out for her hand. She took it, and he picked up their coats and they walked back to the Inn. Their silence was one of expectancy, the tension electric between them. Cavan's arm encircled her and she felt his warm body beside hers, their hips moving together in an increasingly arousing rhythm. Gradually, to her sorrow, common sense began to prevail upon her madness.

When they entered the hallway, Bethany drew her hand from Cavan's. 'Goodnight,' she said as evenly as she could.

'Bethany——' he began in a sensual growl.

'No,' she whispered. 'Goodnight.'

'It was fun.'

'Mmm.' She didn't trust herself to speak.

He stared down at her, his face without expression. After a few interminable seconds he dropped his eyes. 'Goodnight,' he said courteously.

Bethany climbed the stairs numbly. With every step she took, she yearned to whirl around and to invite him with a smile to follow her. Doggedly she plodded on, such a tremendous force compelling her head to turn and look at him that she had to grind her teeth in the effort to resist it.

'I'll be on the yacht if you want me,' he called hoarsely.

Bethany froze, his words knifing through her. 'Is Tania there?' she grated, before she could stop herself.

'I do hope so,' replied Cavan fervently.

Only barely suppressing a strangled cry of rage and frustration, Bethany stumbled up the stairs. The front door slammed soon after, and in a short while she heard the sound of the boat taking him to the waiting Tania. She dragged off her clothes, took the traditional cold shower, thumped her pillow a few times in temper and lay awake for most of the night listening to the complaints of her body.

She dared not let go. She dared not trust him with the strings of her fragile emotions. He was a rover—always had been, always would be. Her heart lurched. She loved a man who was so hungry for sex that he'd never wait for her. And she was too proud to share.

Blearily the next morning she mooched around till a jug full of coffee had revived her. She wanted to stare out at the bay where the yacht bobbed on its mooring as if she'd be able to see into the cabin and know whether Tania had once again triumphed. But she kept her eyes averted.

Finding this more difficult than she expected, she decided to go out. She slipped into an elegant outfit and rang for a taxi to take her to the station and on to Exeter. She returned with an armful of swatches and spent the rest of the day frantically cross-matching patterns and colours, slowly building up an art-board.

Cavan didn't return. Obviously, she thought sourly, Tania was keeping him busy and he was expending some of that boundless sexual energy. She found it hard to sleep that night as well.

Five days had passed and still there was no sign of Cavan. She had almost bitten Mawgan's head off in disappointment when he had telephoned, and she felt horrified and overwhelmingly guilty that she'd offended her brother. She began to jump every time she heard an outboard engine. She found herself hovering by the windows that looked out to sea. She kept falling asleep at odd moments during the day, because she prowled around at night playing loud music to block out the insistent memories of Cavan's hands, his mouth, his voice...

She whirled when she heard the back door open, and ran helter-skelter from the sitting-room into the kitchen. 'Oh. You,' she said rudely to Tania, filled with despair that she'd hoped it was Cavan.

'You look terrible,' said Tania, inordinately pleased.

Bethany bridled, because she'd thought she was looking rather good. She'd dressed in a couture suit in a soft green, since she'd just returned from Truro that afternoon, having found a superb warehouse there which sold four-poster beds. 'You don't like my Valentino outfit?' she asked haughtily.

'I meant those bags under your eyes,' said Tania uncharitably. 'Where's Cavan?'

Bethany blinked. 'What? I don't know. I haven't seen him for...oh, I suppose it must be a few days now,' she said with nonchalance. She knew how long it had been—right down to the hour—but she wasn't intending to let Tania know that.

Tania frowned. 'You haven't?' she squawked. 'I was sure he was with you! I've not seen him all week! He always lets me know where he is in case there's an emergency. And I've got one. A gang of businessmen stranded... Are you *sure* you haven't got him tied up on the bed or something?' she asked suspiciously.

Bethany gave her a scathing look. 'Don't be ridiculous! What would I want to do that for?'

'I can't imagine you'd keep him here any other way.'

Coldly, Bethany stared at Tania. That was a declaration of war, if she ever heard one. 'Go and see if you don't believe me,' she snapped. And then she realised what Tania was saying and that the woman's face was frightened. Bethany's hands suddenly dropped lifelessly to her sides and she stared at Tania aghast. 'Wait a minute!' she cried in alarm. 'He left me on Sunday evening saying he was going off to the yacht. I heard the boat...' Her voice trailed away as she waited hopefully for Tania to confirm that he'd arrived safely that night.

Her hopes were quickly dashed. 'He never turned up,' quavered Tania. 'I waited up for him, too.'

'Oh, my God!' whispered Bethany. 'It was dark. He could have misjudged the tide——'

'Don't be silly,' scorned Tania. 'Cavan can handle any boat anywhere.'

'In that case,' said Bethany, her voice shaking, 'where is he?'

The two women looked at each other, wide-eyed. Bethany saw tears forming in Tania's eyes, and reached out a sympathetic hand. It was roughly shaken away.

'If anything's happened to him, it'll be your fault!' yelled Tania. 'I'm phoning the coastguard.'

Bethany reached the telephone first. 'Wait till I've tried all the numbers he left by the phone,' she frowned, trying to keep a clear head. 'He could be in a number of places. You know how unpredictable he is and how he does things on impulse. You can't call out the coastguard unless you're certain someone's lost at sea.'

She didn't add that after five days' delay it would be too late, anyway. Her heart was thudding and her fingers were so limp and trembling that she could hardly dial the numbers. She drew a blank at the first four. The last one, a number for central London, rang and rang. A lump formed in her throat. She'd have to ring the coastguard, the police... She tried desperately to stay in control and not think of the possibilities. The phone was still in her lowered hand when she noticed that the ringing tone had stopped. With a sharp gasp, she lifted the receiver to her ear.

'Mmm?'

'Cavan?' she squeaked in a high-pitched, disbelieving voice.

'Who the hell's that?' he growled.

'Oh, *Cavan*!' she cried in joyous relief, while Tania wiped away her tears and waited impatiently to know what was happening. 'Oh, I thought you might be drowned! Where have you been? Do you know what trouble you've caused? You said you were going back to the yacht, and Tania said you hadn't turned up and she hadn't seen you for ages, and when I said that I hadn't either——'

'Good grief, Bethany,' he interrupted in lazy amusement, 'you sound as if you've been waiting for me at home like an anxious wife. I hadn't realised I had to report my *every movement* to you. But since I do, here goes... I'm just getting out of bed,' he said, sounding suddenly very husky. 'I'm totally nude. I'm stretching. Now I'm——'

'Cavan!' she snapped, her pleasure rapidly vanishing. 'I don't give a damn what you've been up to or who you've been up to it with. I mean with whom... Oh, *hell*!' she yelled, at his deep laugh. 'You inconsiderate swine! Why don't you go back to bed and do your stretching with whoever you've been snuggling up to?'

'Grammar!' he reproved gleefully. 'You should have said, "With whomever you've been——"'

Bethany slammed the receiver down and glared at it.

'He's alive, I take it,' said Tania drily.

'Don't say anything,' she growled at Tania. 'Don't you dare utter a word.'

'My, my!' murmured Tania, taking no notice. 'Cavan said you still had one hell of a temper on you, and he was right. He sure sets you off, doesn't he? No wonder he grumbles about you so much.'

'I don't know what you're so pleased about,' snapped Bethany, furious with herself for being so childishly cross. 'Cavan's been making whoopee with some female in his London flat. I got him out of bed,' she said tightly. 'At four in the afternoon!' Tania's face fell, and she looked as if she was going to cry again. 'Oh, let's have some tea,' sighed Bethany, her sympathy getting the better of her anger. She reached out and touched Tania's arm. 'You really ought to know that no one will ever tie Cavan down,' she said gently. 'He's the original free spirit.'

Tania glared. 'I'm going to give myself a facial,' she said grumpily. 'Ready for when he comes back. He's too good to give up on.'

Sadly Bethany watched Tania go, and then lost herself in work. By the time she heard Cavan calling from the hall some five hours later, she had calmed down and was in control of herself once more.

A beautiful bouquet of red roses was placed by her colour-board. 'I thought this wasn't the moment for parsley,' he murmured.

She pushed the roses out of her way and carried on working. 'Put them in the bin,' she suggested coldly.

'I couldn't do that,' protested Cavan.

'Flowers won't make me like you. I don't want them.'

'You're not getting them,' he said mildly. 'They're for Tania!'

Bethany clenched her teeth. She could have kicked herself. Now she'd never know if he'd said that just to be difficult! 'Don't interrupt me,' she said, looking as busy as she could. 'I'm concentrating.'

Cavan poured himself a whisky and sat beside her, watching her matching colours and discarding patterns. 'That's nice,' he remarked absently, reaching out for Bethany's favourite material. It was Venetian and cost a small fortune a metre, but she was determined to have it for the main bedroom suite, and would economise elsewhere.

She slapped his hand away. 'Don't move it,' she said curtly. 'I'm seeing if the blue goes with it.'

'Try the champagne,' he suggested. 'Would you like a ticket to the Longchamp races?'

The champagne brocade looked wonderful. 'What for? Did you say Longchamp?' She looked at him suspiciously and blinked in surprise. He was immaculately dressed in a dark business suit, but he looked as if he hadn't shaved for some time, the dark shadow on his jaw unnervingly sexy.

Apparently he'd seen her eyes on his jaw because his hand smoothed it ruefully. 'Sorry about the beard,' he said. He waved his feet at her. 'And the odd socks. I got dressed in a hurry. Longchamp is my next big "do". I have five hundred tickets for the flat race,' he explained. 'I've just done a Tina Turner concert in Hollywood——'

'Oh, yes?' She clipped the brocade to the Venetian sample and hunted for the right gimp to edge the chair she wanted to cover in the fabric.

'God, I'm jet-lagged!' he complained, kicking off his shoes. 'I shouldn't be drinking this.' He stared gloomily at the whisky. 'I'd hoped to get some sleep,' he scowled, 'but I was woken up by some hysterical woman ranting on.'

Bethany studied his face carefully. He did look tired, his whole body slumped, the vitality temporarily depleted. She realised he had probably been jetting around the world after all. 'You could have phoned,' she told him stiffly.

'I had the impression you didn't want to know where I was or what I was doing,' he said soberly.

'I didn't. Tania was worried. You ought surely to keep in touch with your secretary,' she mumbled.

'I'm training her up to handle crises on her own. If she always knew where I was, she'd turn to me for help. Besides, I loathe accounting for my whereabouts to women. I go where I have to, if I have to, when I have to.'

'We were only worried because the boat was gone. Naturally we thought you might have d-d-d...' She couldn't say it. A lump had come to her throat.

'Drowned? Died?' he suggested baldly. Bethany flinched at the physical pain inside her, and Cavan's voice gentled. 'When I left you last Sunday I met some of the fishermen in the bay,' he explained. 'They'd had a bad catch and had given up for the night. We all decided we were fed up and fancied painting Looe red, and we motored up the coast there. The Mackerel Club ran out of beer so we only managed a pink undercoat on the town before everyone went home.' He yawned and gave a rueful grunt. 'I was wide awake and in need of action——'

'You needn't go on,' Bethany said hastily, her imagination working overtime.

He passed a tired hand over his drained face. 'I don't always reach for a woman when I want entertaining,' he said in a soft rebuke. Bethany felt the heat flushing up to her face. It was the word *always* that infuriated her. 'I caught up on my work in London,' he explained wearily. 'Then I went on to Hollywood.'

She bit her lip. 'And I woke you. I'm sorry,' she said in a low voice.

Cavan let out a deep sigh. 'That's OK,' he mumbled, closing his eyes and stretching out his legs luxuriously. 'Oh, God! It's wonderful to be back home. It's all very well being a ticket baron, but Mr Fixit gets tired of rushing around the world ensuring that his clients are satisfied. Talking of satisfaction, that reminds me. Hang on. I'd better ring Tania.'

Bethany let her lashes hide her eyes. Cavan ruffled her hair and strode out. It was over half an hour before he came back, and she was half eaten by jealousy.

'Would you like something to eat?' she asked brightly, trying to make amends.

'My stomach isn't sure what time it is,' he groaned. 'I've crossed so many time zones I'm not even sure of the date. I have to go,' he said reluctantly. 'Tania wants me back.'

'Oh. Perhaps we can discuss my schemes tomorrow some time, when you've recovered,' she said stiffly.

'Mmm.' Cavan rocked on his feet.

She looked at him in alarm. 'I don't like you taking the boat out when you're so tired——'

'Oh, hell!' he frowned, passing a hand over his forehead. 'I forgot. I left the boat at Looe. Damn! I'm too tired to go hacking around borrowing one from a local. Tania will have to lump it. Do you mind if I crash out in the spare bedroom?'

'N-n-no. I'd better ring her, though, and let her know,' she said doubtfully.

'Do that. She's bothered about a client. Tell her she'll have to organise the tickets for the party of stranded businessmen herself. Alitalia owe me a favour, so she can use my name.' He swayed in the doorway.

'I'll fetch some blankets and pillows from the airing cupboard after I've rung Tania,' she said briskly.

Cavan plodded slowly up the stairs. Tania wasn't pleased, but Bethany just gave her the message and rang off in the midst of Tania's protest. Picking up an armful of blankets and topping the pile with a couple of pillows, she went to the spare bedroom.

A gentle smile lit her face. Cavan was face down on the bed, fast asleep, sprawled out as if he'd fallen there. Bethany quietly placed the bedding on the floor and went over to the bed, wondering whether she could remove his shoes without waking him. Gingerly she gripped the soft leather heel of one shoe and slid it off, then the other. Cavan stirred, rolling on to his back.

Bethany's heart somersaulted at his vulnerable, sleep-softened face. His lashes were thick and black, like smudgy crescents on his cheeks, the imperial nose jutting into the air above his slightly parted lips. One arm was flung over his head. His breathing was steady and deep, lifting his ribcage in a regular rhythm. In his sleep he frowned and moved his head as if his tie was constricting his throat.

How she loved him, she thought gently. Her fingers tenderly eased the knot of his silk tie, and she bent over, holding her breath as she attempted to push his top shirt button through the buttonhole. Her tongue slid between her lips in concentration.

'Bethany.'

Her lashes flicked upwards warily, but Cavan was muttering in his sleep. Probably having nightmares, she thought with a wry smile. And then she found herself lying on top of him, trapped by his arm, which he'd brought down over her, the soft skin of her cheek rasped by his beard.

'Cavan!' she whispered, wriggling.

'Mmm,' he grunted, smiling in his sleep and turning over on his side with her wrapped securely in his arms.

Bethany rolled her eyes to the ceiling, wondering what to do. She could wake him—again—but he looked so incredibly contented that she didn't have the heart to do that. She could stay there, or try to prise herself out inch by inch. She went for the latter. He held on to her like a limpet to a rock. It was like a scene in a farce or an old Doris Day movie. Whatever she did, he drew her back to him. If he hadn't been so obviously exhausted and sleeping the sleep of the dead, she would have been highly suspicious.

Exhausted after lack of sleep herself, and from struggling to get free from Cavan's possessive arms, she took
a breather for a few minutes. And promptly fell fast
asleep.

CHAPTER SIX

'WELL, this is nice,' murmured Cavan's voice in Bethany's ear.

Drowsily she registered that he was awake and his bristly chin was rubbing against her jaw. Struggling to consciousness, she drew away from his whispering breath, opening her eyes, which seemed to have been shut.

And discovered that the sun was streaming through the window and it was now morning.

'Oh, no!' she groaned in dismay.

'Do you always sleep with your tights on?' he asked with interest. 'No,' he husked, his voice betraying his pleasure, 'correct that. Stockings.'

'Cavan!' Bethany tried in vain to remove his inquisitive hand from her thigh. Her tight skirt had wriggled right up in the night, exposing the whole length of her long, shapely legs. 'Get your hands off me!' she gasped, wondering what she'd done with her shoes.

'Gorgeous,' he growled. 'I love stockings.' His hand admired them thoroughly while Bethany moaned and complained bitterly. 'Oh, those legs of yours!' he groaned. 'I don't think you ought to writhe around like that,' he breathed jerkily, his eyes heavy with need. 'I'm always *very* sensitive in the mornings.'

His hand slipped to the soft warmth of her thighs between her legs, and Bethany's eyes became huge. 'Please, Cavan!' she croaked.

'All in good time.' He smiled, his mouth drowsy with sleep and sensuality. 'Let me enjoy your body first,' he said huskily, his fingers creeping unnervingly upwards with a slow, inexorable movement.

Bethany jerked in alarm. 'I meant——!' She thought better of speech. Her voice was telling him that his touch was arousing her. Desperate to escape before she was seduced by him, Bethany made a sudden move and rolled off the bed on to the floor. She was on all fours, in the act of rising to her feet, when Cavan landed beside her.

'You're very resourceful,' he grinned, removing her discarded shoe from behind his ear.

'And you're very energetic for a man who's suffering from jet lag,' she retorted shakily, estimating the distance to the door.

He leaned back on one elbow, surveying her. 'I recover quickly. My stamina is legendary.'

She gulped. 'I fell asleep,' she said lamely.

'You seem a little confused,' he soothed.

'I think I'll go and get some breakfast,' she mumbled, half crouching.

'How long are you going to keep running away from me, Bethany?' he asked quietly.

'I'm not running away! I'm trying to avoid you,' she snapped back.

'Same thing,' he laughed. Cavan began to slide his jacket off, and Bethany sidled to the door warily. 'Run, Bethany,' he said in a low growl. 'Run as you always do. You won't confront problems head on, will you?' he taunted. 'You turn tail and take the easy way out.'

'I'm glad that you've accurately diagnosed yourself as a problem,' she said coldly, incensed that he should think she was a coward. 'And you can't claim that I'm running away if I'm staying here and working for you, despite the fact that I find you very irritating.'

'No,' he admitted, 'and you did curl up with me last night. Forgive me for asking, but I can't remember much after I drove down here from London. I can't even remember going up to bed. I hope I didn't miss anything. Did we do anything interesting?'

She looked at him scathingly. 'If we had, you'd know about it,' she said, tossing her head and stalking out to the sound of his rich chuckle.

Bethany went to her bedroom and had a long soak in the bath, ignoring the sounds and smells in the house that indicated Cavan had shaved, showered and dressed, and was now cooking breakfast again for them both. For a macho man, she mused, he was quite handy around the house. Too handy. He never lost an opportunity to touch her, awake or asleep.

As for running away... Her mouth firmed. That was one thing she wouldn't do again. Whatever he did, whatever he threw at her, she'd stick this out and finish the renovation, if only for her own pride's sake. And to see the hotel restored, of course, she thought warmly. She jerked herself out of her reverie and her eyes flashed. Cavan thought he was irresistible and that she'd end up as yet another of his conquests. She'd prove otherwise.

Over the next two weeks, neither of them had much time for anything apart from work. The arrangements seemed endless, but Bethany had a growing suspicion that Cavan was throwing himself into the work as a release for his sexual energies. She welcomed that, their relationship becoming brisk and efficient and utterly impersonal. Bethany the woman didn't seem to exist for him.

She heard his step on the path outside, her ears attuned to his movements. 'I'll put the kettle on,' she said, when he came into the kitchen. Coffee on arrival had become a ritual. Bethany frowned, thinking they had established several rituals together, almost as if they were man and wife.

'I met the postman outside,' said Cavan, waving a large envelope. 'Ah. The architect's plans,' he observed casually, dropping them on to the kitchen table.

Bethany pounced eagerly on them. 'He's taken his time,' she grumbled, examining them carefully. 'Now that's odd!' she declared. 'There isn't a reception area!'

'Er—no.' Cavan came to sit next to her, his face close to hers as he examined the drawings. He smelt fresh and was glowing from his morning shower and the short trip across the bay from his yacht. 'I overruled your instructions there. Too formal.'

'Hmm,' she said doubtfully, but not arguing the point—though the doorkeys had to go somewhere. 'Something else...'

'Y-e-s?' drawled Cavan cautiously.

She flicked him a quick glance. He seemed tense, and she wondered why he was so much on edge. 'I still think we could get more than four bedrooms on the first floor. The bridal suite doesn't really need two settees. Cavan!' she cried in exasperation. 'He's put in a jacuzzi! Was that your idea?'

'They'll get bored with the bed,' he argued. 'I thought we should offer them some alternatives. That's why there's a large area in front of the fire for one of those thick, deep-pile rugs so that——'

'I get the picture,' she said drily. 'You've gone over the top, though. You could put another bedroom in easily if you followed my suggestions. And where,' she queried, searching inside the large manila envelope, 'are the plans for the top floor?'

'Oh, dear. It looks as if he's forgotten them,' said Cavan innocently.

She studied him coolly. 'What are you planning up there?' she asked, her suspicions deepening. 'A brothel for jaded businessmen?'

'You have wonderful ideas,' he said fondly, gazing into her eyes. 'One would almost think you knew exactly how to please a man.'

'Some men are easy to work out. They like anything that satisfies their base lusts,' she retorted caustically. 'Don't try to distract me. I want to see those plans, Cavan. I need to know if you've changed any of the bedroom arrangements otherwise I can't plan the detailed schemes properly.'

'I can't tell you,' he said. 'You're not——'

'Softened up by a night in your arms?' she suggested coldly.

'Trust me——'

'You must be mad. I may be gullible sometimes but I'm not entirely off my head. Those plans had better arrive soon.'

'I'll get on to the architect about them. I can't think how he left them out. Look, let's forget them for the moment. I think I'd like you to concentrate on everything else and leave the top floor till you're sure you can do it up in the time. I'd rather have four bedrooms and all the downstairs ready for Christmas than nothing at all.'

He smiled at her winningly, and she gave him a broad, false smile back and surreptitiously moved her body further away. He had that light in his eyes again and she wasn't taking any risks.

'You're the boss,' she said stiffly.

His laugh sounded a little hollow to her as if it was forced. 'I'll get the plans faxed. Oh, before I forget, are you doing anything special today?' he asked, covering her hand with his.

By now, Bethany knew better than to tussle with him. So she let the hand stay there and gritted her teeth against the way it stroked her skin gently, pretending his touch did nothing to her.

'Depends what you mean by special. The landscape gardeners are coming to begin the pool and level the lawn, I have to keep an eye on the men building the conservatory and I have that chap from the quarry coming with samples of slate for the hall floor,' she said with calm efficiency. 'Other than that, I'm not doing much. Why?'

'I want to help set up the village hall for the harvest festival,' he told her surprisingly. 'While I do that, would you keep an eye out for a large vehicle delivering a medieval staircase and two carved stone fireplaces? I expect you'll hear it bashing down the village street well in advance of its arrival. If it ever gets down,' he added. 'I told them the width of the street, and they promised the lorry would fit. Just.'

'It's not for us, I hope. I didn't order them,' Bethany frowned.

'No. I did—from the architectural salvage people in Bristol. Saw them last week. The staircase and smaller fireplace will be perfect for the hall, and the larger fireplace is to go in the drawing-room. Log fires are very welcoming, aren't they?'

Bethany gave him a sour look. 'You're going over my head again,' she said said tightly. 'You probably haven't measured to see if anything will fit, and I doubt what you've bought will be in keeping. I've a good mind to tell the driver to turn right around when he arrives.'

Cavan's finger touched her lips to silence her protests. 'Give the poor devil a cup of tea first, and have a peek under the tarpaulins. If you don't like what you see the staircase and fireplaces can go straight back,' he murmured. He leaned forwards and dropped a light kiss on her mouth. 'That's for pouting,' he husked. 'I told you not to. Don't mind, do you?'

'Yes,' she said flatly. 'But that won't stop you from annoying me, so I might as well save my breath.' She wiped her mouth deliberately with her handkerchief and persisted with her objection. 'I wish you'd consulted me about the staircase. How much did it cost? A decent one fetches thousands. You'll never get your money back, you know.'

'Thousands? It could have fallen off the back of a lorry, or been stolen from a country house by my gangster friends,' he suggested.

'If I thought you were serious, I'd call the police to investigate,' she said shortly. 'But I know you're only winding me up. I don't want you throwing your money around like this,' she rebuked.

'Do you care if I go bankrupt?' he mocked.

'Not a lot. What does worry me is that you'll sell your half of the building when you discover you can't make any profit running this hotel.'

'Saved by the bell,' muttered Cavan, at the sound of the front door-chimes. 'Good grief! The lorry is early. Come and see.'

Bethany joined him outside, her eyes widening at the sight of the enormous delivery van. 'Where's it going to go?' she asked uncertainly. 'The stuff can't be brought in here and fitted until the slate floor is down——'

'I thought of that,' he said smugly. 'I've bought the disused seine sheds where they used to hang the pilchard nets. Brought a smile to Jory's face!' he grinned. 'Look, I think I'd better lend them a hand,' he said, hurrying to help the gang of men unload the sections of the staircase.

Ever ready with an answer, she thought sourly, running back to answer the telephone. She hastily arranged for the men to plumb in the new en-suite bathroom units, and then became embroiled in a discussion with the gardeners. It was almost two hours before Bethany was able to join Cavan and view the fireplace in all its glory. To her delight, it was a skilfully carved and highly polished oak masterpiece, and it was absolutely perfect for the hall because it would restore its manorial appearance immediately.

'Oh, Cavan!' she breathed, standing in the big doorway of the seine shed. 'It's incredibly beautiful!'

'I'm glad you like it,' he said in pleasure. 'I took a gamble that you would. You wanted a fire in the hall, and now you've got one. There's some panelling to go with it. Linenfold. Yes, it cost me a year's income,' he said impatiently. 'But I had to have it. You must admit it will look fantastic.'

He hugged her in evident glee, and Bethany couldn't help but agree. She wanted to dance about in excitement too. 'I can't wait to see it in place,' she said breathlessly, turning shining eyes on Cavan. 'You're idiotic and impulsive, wildly extravagant and quite crazy, but I love——'

'Me?' he asked, a mocking gleam in his eyes. He sighed when she flinched, but her face immediately lit up again when she looked back at the staircase in all its beauty. 'Bethany...will you do something for me in return?' He chuckled at her wary glance. 'Nothing illegal or immoral!' he grinned. 'Come with me to the harvest festival tonight. I think you ought to start integrating with the villagers a bit. They'll wonder why you avoid them.'

'Tell them it's because I can't bring myself to pretend I'm your girlfriend,' she said lightly. Pretending would be too hard.

'You must make bonds with them,' he insisted. 'Come with me. I can't do much in a crowd of people, can I?'

'No. I don't want to do anything social with you. You'll only use the opportunity to paw me.'

Surprised at the way he flinched, Bethany drew away from him and wandered over to the fireplaces, tracing the stonework carving with her hands. Cavan had remarkable taste—and a bottomless pocket, it seemed. Portallen was being returned to its former glory, and she was part of that transformation. It gave her a happy glow.

'Your old friends will be there,' he coaxed. 'I think you should show your face and let everyone get used to the fact that you'll be here for a while. I can help you, Bethany. Stick with me and I'll get them on your side again. But you have to break the ice. Why not do it under my protection?'

'I don't know.' She hesitated. 'You'll make the most of our supposed relationship and I'll be unable to relax all evening.'

'Until they accept you, you won't be able to ditch me,' he reasoned. 'You're only delaying that. If I didn't know you better,' he murmured, 'I'd think you were keeping up the pretence of our close relationship deliberately, because you rather like the idea of being my girlfriend.'

'Now that is silly,' she said, slight breathlessness in her voice. She cleared her throat. He was right; it would be a good opportunity for her to make a start on establishing her friendships again. She had missed chatting to the people she'd grown up with. 'All right,' she agreed quietly, feeling slightly nervous already. But she'd vowed not to run away from anything—other than Cavan's grabbing hands. 'For my own sake I'll come.'

'Good. I really must go and help them up at the hall. Before I do, there's one thing I ought to warn you about,' said Cavan casually, covering up the staircase and the fireplaces with tarpaulins. 'If anyone asks what's going on down here, just remember that, for the present, we're getting rid of the chrome and glass decoration. It's true, of course. Just don't mention anything about turning Portallen into an exclusive hotel. There could be opposition to that.'

'Are you telling me that they don't know you're upgrading the Inn—and it would be an unpopular move?' Bethany's eyes narrowed.

'Well, there are all kinds of rumours as usual, of course,' he said dismissively. 'Though I get the feeling that everyone would like to see the place restored.'

'They won't be very comfortable drinking in a smart bar,' she said doubtfully. 'Fishy jumpers and sea boots don't exactly look right in exclusive hotels. I'm not sure you're doing the right thing.'

'It's right, surely, to bring the building back to manor-house status. And keep this under your hat, but a local brewery is intending to make an offer on Smugglers' Cottage. It's rambling enough for an atmospheric local, and has been derelict for years. I've suggested a suitable landlord, too. So play it cagey.'

'You've got it all worked out, haven't you? Now tell me why it has to be such a secret,' she said sharply, sensing a fiddle. Perhaps this was why he hadn't let her see all the plans and why he'd been shifty about one or two other points. Like the fact he was looking for one long manorial table instead of a series of smaller ones for the restaurant. They'd argued about that for a long time. 'Is this something to do with income tax?'

'Nothing at all,' he assured her. 'It's merely that I never reveal all my plans to anyone. Natural caution.'

'Well . . . won't the villagers know what's going on? Won't they have seen the request for planning permission in the local papers anyway?'

'Oh, I doubt it,' he said with a disarming smile. 'The truth is that I don't want gossip. You know villagers. Their mouths are as wide as an open-cast mine.'

'I, of all people, know that. You're working some racket,' she accused, her voice hard. 'What is it, Cavan? I demand to know!'

'We have to keep this quiet till I can fix things with the planning department,' he explained with a huge wink. 'They turned me down flat last time I applied.'

She stared, appalled. '*What*?' she cried. 'Are you saying I could do all this work and the whole thing will fall through because you haven't got planning permission yet?'

He strolled to the door, his hands comfortably in his pockets. 'Oh, no,' he said cheerfully. 'I said I'll fix it. Throw around a few free tickets for——'

Her face was a picture. 'You can't!' she cried in horror. 'This isn't that kind of place! What you're suggesting is bribery and corruption!'

'Yes,' he agreed amiably. 'Do you want Portallen done up or not?' He slid quickly out of the door.

For a moment Bethany was rooted to the spot in disbelief. Then, collecting herself together, she ran out, but he had disappeared. Bethany leaned against the seine-house wall, aware that he must have begun to run the moment he stepped outside so that she wouldn't catch up with him. But she'd tackle him that night.

She was furious with him. She didn't want to be involved in anything underhand. Cavan might resort to backhanders as a matter of course, but she could only work for him if everything was above board. All that they'd worked for could be in jeopardy. If Cavan didn't get permission, the Planning Department could legally request that the hotel be restored to its original condition—glass, chrome, open-plan rooms and so on. And that she couldn't bear.

The rest of the day flew by. Bethany had only a brief time to eat and tidy up before she heard Cavan arriving, and she wasn't even half ready.

'Bethany? Leaving in five minutes!' he called up to her.

'Then you'll go alone!' she yelled back, and was disconcerted by the laughter which greeted her reply. It sounded as if he'd brought reinforcements, she thought, hearing the sound of voices and the chink of glasses. Irritably she realised she'd have to wait a little longer to tackle him about the intended bribery of the Planning Department.

In her soft apricot shirt and easy skirt, she ran down the stairs some minutes later. Cavan was in the midst of a crowd of villagers—most of them their old schoolfriends. A momentary frown of annoyance creased her forehead and then she walked forwards with a smile of greeting on her face to hide her nervousness. She gave Cavan a look which indicated that she'd get him later, and he grinned wickedly.

'Here she is!' he said, stating the obvious. 'You look wonderful, Bethany. My favourite outfit.'

He'd never seen it before, she was thinking, and then she was being pressed against his clean white shirt front in a breath-taking hug. She looked up at him with mockery in her eyes. 'Full marks for opportunism,' she said drily.

His kiss took her unawares, and he seemed equally surprised that she didn't push him away. Unwilling to miss his chance, apparently, Cavan became more deeply engrossed in the kiss till a few awkward coughs from the onlookers reminded them both where they were and she emerged dishevelled and confused. Cavan looked triumphant.

'Darling!' He put his arm affectionately around her shoulders, his fingers biting in when she tried to ease herself away from his distracting nearness.

'I reckon we'd better wish you luck,' said Jack Hoskin, his voice lifting at the end of every sentence in the Cornish way. 'You'll need it.' He raised his glass to Cavan, rather obviously excluding Bethany.

'Your happiness, Cavan. Cheers!' All were holding up their glasses now. Except a scowling Tania in the background.

Bethany wondered if she'd wandered into the wrong room.

'They know, darling,' said Cavan with a ruefully apologetic smile.

'Know what, darling?' she asked sweetly, her lashes fluttering ridiculously. He wanted an act, he'd get it, she thought grimly.

He chuckled and bent on the pretext of kissing her ear. Instead he whispered into it. 'I'm afraid they think we're engaged. Can't think how. Don't disillusion them. Play up to it. Darling. Jilt me later.'

She gasped with shock, and there were some sniggers.

'Keep your lewd mutterings for tonight, Cavan!' said Jack. 'You're embarrassing the women here. Hope you've thought hard about this,' he added, looking doubtfully at Bethany as if he disapproved heartily.

'Oh, I have,' smiled Cavan. 'You know I love a challenge. Never happier when there's a rogue fish to land, a bucking yacht without a keel to bring under control, perhaps a wayward animal to master——'

'You're taking advantage of the situation,' muttered Bethany, infuriated by the sly comparisons.

'Later, darling,' he promised her huskily in a stage whisper, as if she'd been murmuring sweet nothings in his ear. He chuckled indulgently and raised his voice so everyone could hear his words. 'We're going to have to get married soon, by the looks of it, or the first of our kids will be illegitimate! It'll be nice to have a Trevelyan family in Portallen again, won't it, darling?'

Bethany felt faint. The cruelty of the situation was hurting her terribly, making her stomach churn. She smiled around brightly, and only Cavan's steadying arm, now firmly around her waist, kept her from crumpling to the floor. That and perhaps the red mist of fury which was sustaining her.

'Children?' she croaked, uncomfortable beneath the faintly hostile stares.

'Our kids,' said Cavan huskily, making Bethany splutter. He patted her heartily on the back. 'Gently, darling,' he said in concern. 'We must watch that cough of yours. I'll give you a Vick rub later.'

'You—you——!'

His fingers squeezed the muscle in her shoulder, relieving her of speech. 'I think it's the plaster dust,' he explained. 'Things are a bit chaotic. There's so much to do in the house.'

'Tell us all about it while we walk up to the hall,' said Jack curiously. 'We're all interested in knowing what you're going to do. Will you change much?'

'Well, there'll have to be a playroom, kids' bedrooms and a nanny's room on the top floor if we're to accommodate our family,' grinned Cavan, propelling the pole-axed Bethany to the door.

'Won't have much room for guests,' mused Jack.

Cavan shrugged. 'The first floor is huge,' he said innocently.

Bethany's mouth had opened in amazement at his quick mind, and she was reluctantly impressed by his brilliant improvisation. He was definitely inspirational at thinking on his feet, and it was an ability she must watch. However, by the time she'd finished with him that night, she thought grimly, he wouldn't be standing on his feet at all. In fact, he wouldn't even know which way up he was.

'Our plans for having children are a very long time in the future. I have no intention of giving up work,' she began.

'That's why we're having an office behind the drawing-room, with two desks facing one another so we can spend the day together,' said Cavan, smiling down on her.

'Isn't that heavenly?' she cried, with saccharine insincerity. His smile broadened at her simpering look. She'd decided that something as twee as two facing desks deserved a suitably vapid response. 'You rat!' she whispered.

'Shark,' he reminded her softly, then spoke to Jack. 'We'll have computer links with my offices around the world, of course. Good, eh? We have our cake and eat it. Portallen, a stimulating business life and...' He gave a husky growl, making everyone laugh, and his sharp white teeth flashed in amusement.

'I'm taking up shark fishing,' Bethany said tartly, flashing her teeth back at him.

'I'll make sure you catch one,' he murmured.

Jack nodded, his manner to Bethany thawing a little. 'Take him up on that, girl,' he urged. 'Cavan's not a bad fisherman for a foreigner.' His voice grew warm. 'And I have to say this; no Portallen fisherman who sets out to sea will ever forget your generosity, nor will his family.'

'Is this something I've missed?' asked Bethany curiously, when she caught Cavan making frantic signals at Jack.

'Dammit, Jack——' he protested.

'You're getting no apologies. It's about time the secret was out of the bag, me 'andsome!' Jack stopped Bethany and pointed to the new coastguard hut. 'There's been a few changes here since you left. First, couple of years back, we had an anonymous donation to buy an Inshore Lifeboat,' he explained.

Bethany stiffened warily, knowing he was referring to her own contribution, and wondering if Cavan had claimed that he'd made the donation. 'Jack, perhaps if you know something about that, you ought to keep it quiet,' she said with a frown.

'I don't hold with that,' said Jack stolidly. 'Not with secrets. Tania's Dad got saved from certain drowning off The Ranneys because the lifeboat was right on hand. She'd have liked to thank whoever donated it, wouldn't you, Tan?'

'Yes. I would.' Tania's face was gentle, and Bethany remembered how much she idolised her father.

It was wonderful, Bethany mused, that her compensation money had been of real use. She felt a warm glow through her body. 'I didn't know, Tania,' she said, putting a hand on her old friend's arm. 'I'm very glad he was saved. I was fond of your father.'

Tania frowned and moved away, to Bethany's disappointment. She had hoped that she could start to mend their relationship.

'Anyway, there's more,' continued Jack. 'Cavan heard the breakwater had been destroyed by the gale, and he paid for it to be rebuilt. After that, the government closed the coastguard down——'

'Closed?' Bethany's eyes rounded. 'But it's still there, modernised and——'

'That was Cavan,' said Jack proudly. 'You got a gem there. You'd better deserve him or you'll have the village to answer to. He got it done privately and I was the only one who knew. Proper job, new building and equipment, monthly salary for someone to man the station,' he revealed while Cavan shifted impatiently. 'I got the job. I'd been out of work for a year. Cavan can't do no wrong, far as I'm concerned, and sooner the village knows the whole truth the better, to my mind.'

'I'm stunned,' said Bethany honestly, and so, it seemed, was everyone else. They began to chatter and show their appreciation of Cavan's generous gesture. She began to smile ruefully to herself. Cavan had used his money for the public good... or... Her mind raced and she reluctantly considered the alternative. Was it a carefully calculated backhander from him to ensure that no one in the village raised any objection to his development of the Inn?

'I can see your brain working,' murmured Cavan.

'I hope you're suitably worried, then,' she said sweetly, 'I'm planning something spectacular for you as a reward for being so smart.' She drew away from his grasp and walked to the village hall on her own while the others crowded around Cavan to discuss Jack's revelation.

Standing in the old hall, which looked smaller than it used to, she felt a warm glow purely because she was beside Cavan. The friendship and welcome shown to him rubbed off on her, and she enjoyed the harvest festival more than any she could remember. The hall was a glorious sight, filled with banks of vegetables, bread baked in the shape of wheatsheaves, home-made preserves and armfuls of country flowers.

After the simple service, and with the rafters still ringing with the vigorous sound of the fishermen's choir and their rendering of 'Harvest Home', Bethany left on Cavan's arm, a lucky corn dolly for the Inn held tightly in one hand. Smiling faces beamed in his direction, men slapped him on the back. Word had got around about his generosity. It worried her that he was so popular. If she jilted him now, everyone would take his side. Cavan was more admired than ever. It would be impossible to leave him without earning the undying hatred of everyone in Portallen. She'd have to wait till the euphoria died down a little, or she'd never succeed in breaking down the barriers.

'How about a nightcap?' Cavan called to everyone in earshot.

Bethany was deafened by the enthusiastic response. 'Aren't you overdoing the generous Mine Host bit?' she muttered to him. She was finding it quite a strain, coping with his affectionate glances, and the thought of a few more hours of being caressed by his hands, his eyes, his voice, was too unnerving to contemplate.

'Careful, Bethany. You're supposed to adore me.'

'Oh, is that it? You want to show everyone how deeply affectionate we are! If you think——'

'Smile. Don't turn nasty on me in front of all these people, or you'll find it hell to work here for the next few months.' His ruthless eyes met hers mockingly as they set off down the cobbled street.

She took a deep breath. 'I think I know this scenario. This is where I plaster myself all over you and make goo-goo eyes at you, is it?' she asked through her inane smile.

'Please yourself,' he said amiably, helping her to keep her balance on the big, uneven cobbles. 'Me, I'm going to milk this situation for all I'm worth.'

'Since you're worth nothing, you won't get much out of it, then,' she retorted sourly.

'Let's see, shall we?' he retorted smugly. In the darkness of the street, he bent his head and kissed her, his eyes dancing wickedly as she glared at him and kept her mouth hard beneath his forceful lips. 'Respond, damn you!' he muttered.

'I won't——' Too late, she realised he'd intended her to speak. It meant he could slide his tongue into her mouth, and she was having to steel all her nerves against the erotic sensation as he explored her mouth with a slow, lingering pleasure.

'Fair,' he said, lifting his head, with the others now tactfully far ahead of them. 'But I'll have to give you plenty of lessons. You hardly aroused me at all.'

'That was my intention, you swine!' she whispered.

'Oh, dear. You do keep getting your animals muddled up,' he said fondly, releasing her but keeping a firm grip on her wrist.

'Roll on Christmas,' she grated furiously when he hurried her down the street to catch up the others.

'Nights before a roaring fire, opening Christmas stockings, wearing paper hats and pulling crackers?' he hazarded.

Her lips compressed at the brief stab of knife-blades in her heart at the cosy scene. 'Yes,' she said grimly. 'With me in Bodmin and you somewhere—anywhere—else.'

'You'll get your wish,' he said quietly. 'I'm going to Brittany tomorrow, then Paris, then Hawaii.' He assessed her reaction with calculating eyes.

For a few seconds, her overwhelming disappointment showed, and then she had covered it up with a bright smile, quite perplexed by the sadness that had descended on her. She didn't want him to go. The place would be like a ghost village without him.

'How long for?' she faltered.

'Want me back quickly?' he asked huskily.

Bethany flushed. Yes, she said fervently to herself. 'No!'

'You don't sound too sure.'

'I am, I am,' she answered irritably, incapable of preventing her mouth from drooping and betraying her innermost longings.

Amusement softened his cynical features and his eyes laughed openly at her. 'I think we'll turn this into a night to remember,' he murmured. 'Tania!'

Tania sullenly turned around to look at Cavan, the big gold buttons on her scarlet blouse glinting under the streetlamp. 'What?'

'Party?' smiled Cavan engagingly.

Tania lit up and she ran to Cavan, taking his arm. 'Party, everyone!' she called to the others.

With whoops of delight, they all poured into the bar, keeping Jack and Cavan constantly busy serving drinks 'on the house'. Towards Bethany there was a strained politeness. No one really trusted her, and they didn't seem ready yet to abandon their long-held beliefs that she was 'fast' and definitely undesirable to have around. She felt very much the outsider, and remembered wryly that once Cavan had been an outsider. Now she knew how he'd felt, thrown into the deep end, introduced to a new family, new surroundings, a new way of life.

He'd coped. So would she. Bethany smiled at one of her old schoolfriends and received a faint smile in return. She could have hugged the girl for giving her hope. It might take her a while, but she'd eventually get accepted again—of that she was certain.

'We're dancing.'

Bethany looked up at hearing Cavan's arrogant order, and saw the warning light in his eyes. Chairs were being pushed back and a romantic ballad was being relayed from the music-centre behind the bar. She shrugged, knowing she couldn't avoid close contact with him, and slid into Cavan's encircling arms. No—melted into them, she thought hazily, bemused by the music and warm glow of happiness which kept surfacing.

Perhaps it was because he was gazing down at her so lovingly in his award-winning act of a man infatuated with his fiancée. Or because he was leaving soon and she wanted to make the most of this evening. Perhaps it was because his personal approval was easing the hostility she'd come to expect and it was a joy to feel the first few grudging acknowledgements that she existed and wasn't a two-headed monster.

'Our engagement is having some results.'

'What?' she asked Cavan, a little disconcerted. She'd been thinking how lovely it was to be held securely by him.

He chuckled deeply, the sound resonant in her own body. 'You're not getting such wary glances from the women, now they think you're tied up with me. I suppose they imagine you've got your hands full and won't play around with their men. Let's convince them a little more, hmm?'

Silent in his embrace, Bethany allowed him to draw her close and hold her against his heart. Her body shaped to his as if it had been formed especially for him. Cavan growled in his throat but he did nothing more than hold her and let their bodies sway to the rhythm. It was enough for Bethany. More than enough.

Someone turned the lights down. In the semi-darkness, she found herself wishing the pretence could go on for a long time. It meant she could touch and be touched without Cavan's cynical smile of triumph coming between them.

'Beth,' he murmured.

She quivered. He had adjusted his body imperceptibly and his hand had clamped on her lower back and pushed her hips hard towards him. Until then she hadn't known she'd been keeping a distance between her hips and his. Now she did. Her face flamed when she felt the hardness of his arousal against her.

'I want to sit this one out,' she breathed, the cruel, spiralling need hurtling through her body with a ruthless and dizzying speed.

His wicked eyebrow lifted in amusement. 'You can't leave me on the dance-floor in this state,' he said in a deep growl. His lips nuzzled her earlobe. 'They'll wonder what you've been promising me.'

He thought of nothing but sexual pleasure. With an effort she kept her temper and her head. He was building up a huge backlog of situations which needed a suitable vengeance, she thought angrily. 'You're not doing this for me at all, are you?' she said miserably. 'You're hoping I'll enjoy being your girlfriend so much that I'll let you whisk me off to your bed.'

'That's very true,' he admitted huskily. His hand slid to rub gently at the nape of her neck. 'I can hardly deny what you're doing to me, Bethany.'

'To what extent have you set all this up?' she asked, hoping she sounded indulgent. To put him off the scent, she arched more firmly against him, and was rewarded by his shuddering gasp. So she did have some power over him, then, she thought in wonder.

'Oh, Beth, I want you!' he whispered. 'I have to have you!'

His mouth descended to hers, bruising in its predatory hunger. She let her hands twine around his neck, gripping his hair tightly as he savaged her mouth. For a few seconds she responded, yielding to the unbearable urge to surrender. And then she pulled back.

'People,' she mumbled, running her tongue over her swollen mouth. 'Too public... Cavan, you arranged everything to get me here, to bring me to this moment, didn't you?' she asked again, her heart thudding as she waited for his answer.

'I must confess I did,' he said in a low tone.

Bethany barely managed not to tear him limb from limb. 'How far back?' she asked huskily, stroking the back of his neck.

'When I started putting the pressure on Mawgan. Almost everything that came after that was planned. I wanted you so much,' he said helplessly.

Want, she thought bleakly. She was only an ache in his body, that unfulfilled conquest, an unmastered woman. The fish that got away. She clenched her jaw. She was planning her own arrangements for his comeuppance. And it would mean sailing so close to the wind that she might end up drowning. She'd hit him in his vanity.

'I'm impressed,' she said softly, her hand stroking his big chest.

'You're not going to hurl abuse at me?' he asked shakily, his voice very husky.

She slid her hand beneath his jacket, caressing his body. Cavan's breath sounded heavy and uneven in her ear. She might not be able to reach him any other way, but she could reach him through his overweening ego, she thought resentfully.

'It's rather a compliment,' she sighed, laying her cheek against his. His heartbeat juddered unevenly, matching hers, and she fought for control, knowing she had to stay clear-headed.

'I had to do something to get you,' he smiled.

She shook with rage and turned it into a sensual wriggle. It electrified Cavan. His hands were everywhere in the half-darkness, the drugging rhythm of his surreptitious fingers crawling inexorably to her breast, softly throbbing beneath the fabric of her shirt.

He took her face between his hands, kissing her forehead, her nose and her lips so tenderly that she wanted inexplicably to cry. Her eyes darkened and she felt a crazed wanting surge up inside her to threaten her composure.

She told herself severely that he'd set her up—and Mawgan. The relentless pressure on her brother, getting her back to Portallen, wheedling his way into the villagers' good books, blackmailing her to stay by using her old home as a lure, and 'accidentally' ensuring that people thought they were engaged.

All because he had to have her. He was unswerving in his pursuit. Consumed with lechery. Pitiless in his drive to be the boss. He'd sworn to 'have her' as if she were some prize to be wrenched from a trophy stand. She took a deep breath. He didn't even consider that he might hurt her in the process.

'You want me?' she husked.

'You know I do.'

There was something savage about his answer, and Bethany felt afraid. Her eyes widened as she became alert to what she was intending to do; to lead him on and then—at the crucial moment—reject him. Her hand explored the muscles of his chest. Forcing a small, flirtatious smile, she allowed her fingers to drift to his biceps. His latent strength daunted her.

In a blinding flash she realised that she'd been kidding herself. Even if she did manage to withstand his remorseless seduction, he'd never let her escape. There was a tension in his body which was almost menacing, a barely controlled violence that would erupt and engulf her if she attempted to thwart him. Cavan wasn't a boy to be turned down. He was a grown man who always got what he wanted.

And he looked as sure as hell that he'd get it tonight.

Bethany was terrified at what she'd done. She couldn't go through with it. Cavan held her close, and they barely moved to the music, swaying dreamily like some of the other loving couples to the sensual music. But her mind was whirling as she attempted to find a way out.

She could faint—but why? She could have a row with him, but people would probably side with him, not her. What it needed was a public and overwhelmingly powerful reason for her to be angry with him. But what? She needed time and space and peace to think, without Cavan's distracting presence. She must extricate herself from Cavan's trap before she was emotionally destroyed.

'Cavan,' she husked, 'I need to powder my nose.'

'You're not running away, are you?' he asked quietly.

'No. I swear on my honour that I'll be back in a few moments,' she said shakily.

'Darling. You're as keyed up as I am,' he murmured, letting his finger trace her soft, trembling mouth. She gasped, and he pushed her away. 'Go, but hurry back,' he said hoarsely. 'I'll see if I can persuade these people here that they're all playing gooseberry.'

'Cavan!' came Tania's sharp voice. 'I need to speak to you!'

Bethany paused, wondering why Tania looked so white, and sensing that her old friend was on the edge of her temper.

'Not here,' said Cavan curtly, 'and not now.'

'Yes, now!' hissed Tania. 'I won't stand by and see you make a fool of yourself. Are you blind? Don't you see what's in front of your eyes?' Her hands ran lightly down her soft blouse, almost as if by accident, drawing Cavan's attention to her generous breasts.

Distressed, Bethany realised that Tania had not given up her ambition to hook Cavan. He stood stock still, sweeping Tania with a slow look. Bethany saw how she bloomed beneath his glance, her lips pouting seductively, her breath shortening so that her chest heaved and strained the large gold buttons fastening the lacy blouse.

'Tania,' he began, his eyes apparently reluctant to leave Tania's sexy body. She wriggled seductively, and Cavan obviously was incapable of resisting the invitation. 'OK,' he said, capitulating with unseemly haste. 'Now. Outside. Five minutes. Bethany——'

'I think I'll turn in now,' she cut in in a chilly voice. 'Say goodnight to everyone for me. Goodnight, Cavan.' Quickly, before he realised what she was doing, she leaned forwards and pecked him on the cheek, moving hastily out of his reach again.

'Is that it?' he asked quietly. 'A cool goodnight? Will your bedroom door be locked against me?'

She reeled at his nerve. 'Definitely,' she answered, her eyes blank.

'I'm not waiting, Bethany,' he frowned. 'Not any longer. I've done all the waiting I intend to do.'

Grimly he took Tania's arm and pushed her outside, leaving Bethany with all the wind taken out of her sails. There was a terrible sick feeling in her stomach. By rejecting him, she'd driven him directly into Tania's willing arms. He was a passionate male with basic needs who'd hoped for an end to the physical hunger he'd been unwillingly suffering. He'd had enough of the starvation diet—he needed sex, now, tonight. And if Bethany wasn't going to provide that, he was determined to let her know that there were plenty of women who would. Tania happened to be around.

Five minutes. Bethany knew he'd be making his pitch, flirting, propositioning, perhaps kissing Tania. He had every right to, of course. He was fancy-free, since their engagement was a farce. She winced at the thought.

Instead of going straight upstairs as she'd planned, Bethany stayed on the fringe of the party, miserably sipping a drink at the bar. She dared not admit that she was waiting for Cavan to return—and that she half dreaded how he might look. Satisfied? Smug? Dishevelled ...?

For the tenth time she checked her watch. They'd been gone for twenty minutes, and suddenly she could take her self-torture no longer. She slipped up the stairs, her legs trembling, and sat down on the bed. She'd known the kind of man he was. This should have come as no surprise. Yet being confronted so cruelly with the truth was still a shock. Somewhere inside she'd believed Cavan to be decent and sincere, to have more depth and tenderness than any man she'd ever met. It was a devastating blow to discover that she'd been wrong.

Bethany groaned. She got up and went over to the window, opening it to take a deep breath of air before she went downstairs again. There was a knock on the door.

'It's locked!' she yelled.

'It's me!' called Tania. 'Someone on the phone for you. Cavan's phone, in the car.'

'Oh!' Bethany jumped up. 'Who would—is it Mawgan?' As she opened the door, she heard the sound of feet on the stairs and caught a brief glimpse of Tania disappearing into the bar again.

With a puzzled frown, Bethany ran down to the car and flung open the driver's door, leaning in to reach for the handset. When she picked it up, however, the caller had rung off. Disconsolately she replaced the receiver and, as she did so, her hand came to rest briefly on something hard on the driver's seat. Her fingers closed around the object and she knew immediately what it was.

The whole of her body stilled down as if it had been chilled in ice. Slowly her fingers uncurled to reveal one of the gold buttons from Tania's blouse. Attached to the button was a piece of material as if it had been... Her eyes glazed. As if it had been impatiently ripped off by someone in a hurry. At that moment, as if to underline more thoroughly what had happened, Bethany became aware of a lingering perfume filling the inside of the car. Tania's perfume.

Her head lifted and she stared unseeingly into space. Cavan had gone further than she'd thought, faster than she'd imagined. She'd wanted a reason to jilt him in public; now she had it. And she wished she hadn't.

CHAPTER SEVEN

BETHANY felt as if someone had thrust her into an ice-box, she was so cold, frozen into immobility. Then something snapped in her brain and she ran to the jetty, flinging the button away from her into the sea as if it burnt a hole in her hand. Stumbling across the courtyard, she rushed blindly, hysterically into the bar.

Everyone looked up in surprise when the door slammed open and Bethany stood, dishevelled and scarlet-faced, her enormous eyes accusing Cavan. The faces became a blur, the whispers fell to silence. The focus of her whole attention was on his cheating eyes.

She took a deep, shuddering breath. 'You—you—*bastard*!' she croaked. 'You lying, cheating, two-timing——'

His eyes pierced into her. 'What——? What are you playing at, Bethany?' he growled menacingly, tensing his body for a fight.

'Evidence!' she cried miserably. 'Of your deceit, your lies! Oh, Cavan! How could you? I thought——' She broke off, unable to continue, only dimly aware of the muttering around her. They faced one another, a white line around Cavan's mouth and hot ice in his eyes. Whereas she was distraught, as any woman who had found firm evidence of someone else in the life of the man she loved would be. She looked around for Tania. She wasn't there.

'What evidence?' he asked flatly. 'What are you trying to do, Bethany? You're making it up——'

'No!' she cried wildly. 'Do you think I'd be reacting like this if I were?'

'God! You might,' he answered, so low that she could hardly hear him, 'if you were trying to find an excuse to jilt me.'

Her face was pale, the trembling of her lips and hands the only visible signs of movement about her. Ironically, she knew that if she had tried to deceive him she would have failed. Cavan was so sharp-witted that any false, invented accusation would have been laughed away. But he could see—*anyone* could see—that she was not acting, that she was genuinely shocked.

Why, she didn't know. She'd been aware of Tania from the start. It was seeing something tangible of his promiscuity that upset her. 'Oh, Cavan,' she said brokenly, letting all her sadness spill out, 'you've hurt me. I thought—I—oh-h!' She burst into tears.

'Hold it!' roared Cavan, his eyes blazing in his white face. 'Get out, everyone,' he said through his teeth, trying to control himself. 'I want to be alone with Bethany.'

'Don't leave me!' she pleaded to the group.

'As God is my witness,' snarled Cavan, 'if you won't leave I'll make you, one by one!'

'Now look here, boy——' began Jack.

'Don't "boy" me!' growled Cavan. 'Bethany has staged this. I don't know how and I don't know why. One of her jokes, probably. But you all know what there is between us, and you damn well owe it to us both to let me sort it out.'

Bethany grabbed hold of a chair and dragged it to her, sitting down, her legs giving way. Embarrassed, people began to leave, a deadly silence over the room. All she could think of was that Cavan had been making love to a woman in his car as if he were an adolescent boy who couldn't wait till a more discreet time and place presented itself. The last person left, and she was alone with Cavan.

She put her head in her hands and then found herself jerked to her feet. Her eyes lifted up to meet Cavan's in fear. She could smell the blistering anger pouring from him. His eyes were as cold and hard as hot sapphires, the hostility leaping between them.

'What is this evidence?' he asked, his face savage.

Her vocal chords wouldn't work. She croaked something, and he shook her impatiently. 'S-something belonging to another woman that I found on the s-s-seat of your car,' she pushed out through parched lips.

His mouth tightened. He swept her up bodily into his rough arms, a savage expression on his face, and began to stride to the stairs, anger carrying him forwards while she struggled ineffectually, almost incapable of breathing because of the way he was ruthlessly imprisoning her in his hard, unyielding, unloving arms.

'No, you didn't, Bethany. I'm going to get the truth out of you,' he threatened grimly, 'if I have to shake every syllable out of those lying lips.'

Frantically Bethany wriggled in his grip. 'You won't hurt me,' she rasped, trying to convince herself.

'Won't I?'

Her apprehensive eyes saw the sharpening of the bones of his face. Cavan was ferociously angry. Panic robbed her of the ability to move, to plead for sense to prevail, to beg him to stop and listen to her explanation. He carried her to her bedroom and hurled her on to the bed. This was a Cavan she had never seen, had always suspected lay beneath the surface, but had subconsciously dreaded knowing. A man whose only intention was revenge for the public shattering of his pride.

'I...' Desperately she sought to lubricate her arid throat, her lips shaping words which never emerged.

'You bitch,' he said in a soft, harsh growl. 'How dare you try to destroy my reputation? I suppose this was the spectacular reward you'd been planning for me. You even warned me it was coming. You thought that making some false accusation would let you off the hook, didn't you?' he breathed. 'If I wasn't so damn sure that I haven't made love to a woman in that *particular* car,' he said with an emphasis that made her jerk with anguish, 'you might have got away with it. As it is, you've hit the penalty clause.' He surveyed her cynically and began to ease off his tie.

Bethany's eyes grew enormous. 'Pen-pen——' She scrambled up the bed at the look in his eyes. 'No, no, *no*!' she choked, finding her voice at last. 'You won't! You can't! You daren't!' Cavan flicked his top shirt button undone then eased the links from his cuffs and threw them carelessly across the room. 'It's not what you think!' She knelt up to plead with him, but Cavan continued to undo the buttons of his shirt with slow and menacingly deliberate movements.

'Isn't it?' he asked harshly. 'You gave a very convincing performance down there.' Her eyes swept downwards in shame, but her chin was clamped between his bruising finger and thumb and jerked sharply up. 'Now you're going to give another kind of performance,' he seethed.

She quailed at the ruthless glitter in his eyes. 'No! You've no right to be angry! You're the one who's in the wrong; you and Tania . . .' She swallowed at the look on his face.

'Tania? You think——' His breath hissed out in exasperation. 'I went out to talk to her——'

'In your car!' she flung.

'Sure. Tan said she was cold.'

'I'm not surprised, if you'd ripped her blouse open.' Appalled at her words, torn from her by violent jealousy,

Bethany hung her head in shame. Cavan forced her to behave in an uncivilised manner, she thought resentfully.

'That's going to be your story, is it?' he asked grimly. 'You're actually going to implicate one of your oldest friends without caring what the consequences might be for her?'

'I'm telling the truth and you know it——'

'If you haven't been putting on a show and pretending I've outraged your honour, then why are you upset?' he frowned. 'What do you care if I make love to another woman?'

'I—I...' Bethany desperately tried to think of a reason.

'There's no answer to that, is there?' he said, his eyes glittering. 'Because my reading of the situation was correct in the first place. You calculated the best way to humiliate me.'

'No!' she cried, panic making her incapable of thinking straight. 'When I went to your car to answer the phone, I saw I needn't have bothered. The evidence had been there all the time.'

'The phone? Is that what you've just thought of as an excuse to be in my car? Sorry,' he said coldly. 'It won't wash. I know you're lying. And if there's anything I hate more than a cold-hearted, calculating bitch it's one who lies to me and tries to shame me in front of my friends. Tania aside, what do you think you've done to my pride, to my character? I've had a good name in this village.' He clenched his jaw. 'You've tried to ruin that.'

'You can't keep this up,' she breathed. 'You know you're guilty! I know you are! You're trying to keep your so-called "good name" at my expense because I'm the one who has been gossiped about and you think you can make the mud stick again.'

'I've heard enough,' muttered Cavan. 'You have an answer every time. Lies, lies, lies. I can't tell you how

angry I am, and how disappointed that you should stoop
to such a low trick. I'm going to do what I should have
done a long time ago, and in doing so I'll prove to you
that I couldn't possibly have made love to a woman half
an hour previously.'

Bethany groaned. Her nerves were skittering around
chaotically. Cavan's body seemed to fill the whole room,
looming menacingly in front of her, his broad shoulders
emphasised in silhouette. His face was in shadow and
he seemed frighteningly primitive in his rage.

'If you assault me——' she husked. The shirt dropped
to the floor. His hand went to his belt, and Bethany drew
in a sharp breath which shuddered right through her.
'*No!*' she breathed.

He had no mercy, no gentleness now. The man who'd
flown the kite and fooled around had vanished. This was
the raw, hurting Cavan, who never let anyone get away
with a slight, who fought back, measure for measure,
blow for blow, whenever he was attacked.

'I'm not going to assault you,' he muttered, his hand
on the zip of his trousers.

She averted her head. 'Rape?' she whispered.

Cavan's nostrils had scrolled scornfully, but he said
nothing. Yet to Bethany his eyes had been eloquence
enough, telling her of his hate and of his determination
to see her crushed. 'Crawl, damn you, crawl!' he'd raged
at her that time they'd quarrelled so publicly. Her teeth
drove into her lower lip. Here in her own bedroom she
was defenceless.

Out of the corner of her eye she was aware that he
was half naked, the blurred, tanned image ruthlessly im-
pressing itself on her fevered brain.

'Look at me,' ordered Cavan.

She shook her head mutely and tipped her head back
in despair. 'Have pity on me!' she whispered.

'You've gone too far,' he rasped. 'Before I leave for my trip I have to seal this intolerable, painful, inescapable bond between us. If I don't, God knows what you'll do, where you'll go.'

Her ankles were grabbed, and with a scream she found herself drawn out full length on to the bed. Cavan lowered his body on to hers, and she shrank into the mattress at the intensity of the heat burning through her, right through her clothes. He lifted her arms over her head and studied her face.

'There is no bond. You'll have to force me,' she grated. 'You won't have the satisfaction of surrender.'

'Oh, yes, I will,' he said arrogantly. He kissed her sullen mouth, and she wrenched her head away, but it didn't matter to him that she was trying to avoid his touch. 'But I don't think I'll get anywhere by forcing you. There are better ways,' he said with a softly sensual threat. 'More enjoyable. Ones which will give me physical and mental satisfaction. To hear you begging, to know you're ready to *crawl...*' His mouth searched warmly over her neck.

Bethany kept herself rigid, suffering in silence. When his hands reached up to undo the buttons of her shirt, she struggled to stop him, but he was remorseless, his fingers roughly and skilfully laying her body open to his hungry eyes.

'Please don't shame me,' she whispered.

'You're beautiful,' he breathed, resolutely ignoring her. He kissed the skin below her collarbone with a delicate brushing of his lips that made her quiver through and through. She smelt the warmth of his hair, felt it across her mouth, the glossy strands clean and fresh. Gradually Cavan's barely controlled anger subsided completely and desire took over. His kisses became more seductive and caressing, and she found it harder and harder with every second to stand the touch of his lips and the grazing sensation of his teeth over her shoulders.

He was too practised a lover, too well-versed in women's likes and dislikes for her to loathe what he was doing, and that filled her with despair. He *wouldn't* succeed in making love to her; that would be her ultimate defeat.

'*I hate you*!' she whispered with a sudden ferocity.

'Fine,' he said harshly. 'Any reaction is better than none. So go ahead. Hate me.'

More ruthlessly, his mouth covered hers, surrounding her parted lips, and the warm moistness of his tongue sent a tremor through her receptive body.

'Oh, Cavan, you don't know what you're doing,' she moaned.

'I do,' he growled. 'I'm rolling back the years. I should have done this before you married and changed the course of our lives.' His eyes glowed and his voice dropped to a low, husky growl. 'If I'd made love to you then, my obsession with possessing you would, perhaps, be over. You might not despise me so much as you do now. So let's pretend. You're eighteen and crazy about boys. You're teasing me, flirting, hungry for a man's touch.'

Bethany closed her eyes and felt a light kiss on each lid. Imagining they could turn the clock back was cruel. 'You can't—ohh!' she groaned in sheer carnal pleasure.

He had tantalisingly allowed his fingers to trail down her arms and then had lifted himself slightly so that he could see and touch her breasts. They sprang into life, anticipating his touch with a deep, throbbing need. She made no attempt to stop him. She couldn't. The sensation was too intense and too welcome. So, with triumph on his face, he brought her breasts to such a hard fullness that she could hardly hold down her need to wriggle and relieve the spasms in her womb created by his hands and his mouth curving around her swelling, voluptuous flesh.

'Warm. Sweet to taste, to touch, in my mouth, beneath my hands...'

'I'll sue you for all you've got,' she husked in a last desperate attempt to hold back. 'Assault. Rape——'

'No chance. You'll be willing,' he repeated. He licked his lips. They parted. They enclosed one throbbing nipple, and she gasped in sheer delight at the tiny quivers of heat which coursed into her loins and filled her body with weak lassitude.

This wasn't rape. It was wonderful seduction, everything she'd dreamed of, and she could no longer resist. Cavan growled huskily in his throat, nursing at her breast, his eyes closed in rapture. Barely knowing what she was doing, she took his head in her hands and gently moved him to her other starving breast, and she settled into the mattress with a sigh at the sweet tugging sensation as he obediently suckled there.

'Cavan,' she mumbled, half in despair, half dreamily. Her hand lightly stroked his dark hair. And then it stilled. He was caressing her hip, and within her body there was a feeling like hot red wine, her head as dizzy as if she'd drunk a whole flagon.

'I didn't make love to Tania. Can't you tell that?' he murmured. She didn't want to answer—or to tell him that she was beginning to believe what he was saying. 'You're gorgeous,' he husked. 'Soft, silken, probably wickedly expensive, but what the hell.'

'No, I——'

She found that her protesting mouth was claimed again, but this time more fiercely, and he groaned softly as she clung to him, straining up to feel the strength of his powerful body. Her skin was humming, tingling, beneath the onslaught of his exploring lips.

'The shadow of your throat,' he murmured, kissing
the hollow tenderly. 'The curve beneath your breast...'

Bethany jerked spasmodically as his tongue left a moist
path there. She heard a rustling and reached down to
clutch frantically at her skirt, her eyes frightened. It had
been so long since she'd made love. Too long.

'Oh, no, Cavan,' she pleaded hoarsely.

'But you are beautiful,' he crooned, covering her body
with kisses. 'Every inch, every curve and valley.' His voice
ended in a croak as he surveyed her lying there beneath
him. 'Sweetheart,' he whispered thickly, 'I've waited so
long for this. I even left Portallen because of you.'

'What?' She frowned uncomprehendingly. She shuddered. Cavan was stroking her hip lightly, rolling his
fingers over her flat stomach, and she gritted her teeth,
trying to push his hands away.

'You were driving me crazy even then,' he whispered,
kissing her sweetly. 'You matured far too early. It was
disturbing, having you around in the same house, wan-
dering about in your underwear with that fabulous body
already like a woman's. I had to get out, or find myself
in gaol! Oh, Bethany,' he groaned, his weight pressing
hard down on her.

Her head spun. He'd wanted her. With a groan, she
lifted her arms to his neck and dragged his head down
so that she could kiss him hard and rid herself of some
of her terrible need.

'Bethany,' he muttered, 'it's ironic it should end like
this. I went to London to make a fortune so that I could
come back and impress you, perhaps dazzle you into
bed.'

Her mouth paused in its demands. He'd wanted her
that much? They could have been lovers, perhaps for
months, a year... Her fingers found his shoulders and
she pushed. Cavan drew back and looked down on her.
'You really wanted me?' she asked shakily.

His blue eyes pierced into her. 'When I came to claim you, I was too late,' he said flatly. 'Dan had you.'

She flinched. Tears filled her eyes. Her head turned helplessly to one side, and then she felt Cavan's weight leave her. Listlessly she heard sounds which told her he was dressing hurriedly.

And then there was a long silence. Miserably she looked around and saw he was sitting on the end of the bed, his back to her. He couldn't leave her now, she thought with an inner moan. How could he? She was unbearably aroused.

'You're cruel,' she whispered wretchedly.

'Because just in time I remember your late husband and find it hard to trespass on his property?' he asked harshly.

'I think I'd better tell you about Dan,' she breathed, fumbling for her shirt and drawing it on.

'Thanks,' he said curtly, 'but I'd rather not know.' His hand banged down on the bed. 'Yes, dammit, I would! It might take away this ache, this violent need I have to make love to you! It might make me sane again and let me get on with my life!' He twisted around, scowling at her flushed, love-softened face. 'God!' he groaned. 'Do you think I could be interested in Tania when my mind is totally taken up with you?'

'Oh, Cavan!' she said brokenly. 'You...' She bit her lip. He'd said nothing about loving her. Only need. Male pride, male desire.

'You made me what I am. Successful. You were scornful of me, and that got me right where my pride lives. I worked night and day to prove to you that I could make it on my own, that a Cockney kid was as good as you proud Celts in Cornwall. I was going to show you the flat I'd bought, take you around the West End. And you robbed me of that pleasure when you calmly announced that you were getting married!'

'I didn't know I'd hurt you so deeply,' she mumbled. 'We all admired you——'

'And no one ever told me, ever showed it,' he said tightly. 'There was a grudging respect from the men here, perhaps, but a reserve, too, and they were so darned sure I was going to take their girls and women that I was never accepted as a friend. I was closer to you than anyone. We touched, even if it was in anger half the time. And then you left.'

'Dan and I——' The words stuck in her throat. Cavan had needed her, and she hadn't seen that. Her eyes filled with tears because she couldn't tell Cavan what she felt about him, and to hell with the anguish it would cause her when he'd had enough of her.

'OK,' he said, his face harrowed. 'It's too painful for you. I get the message.' He stood up, and Bethany saw to her astonishment that he was shaking. Angrily he grabbed the back of a chair and scowled at the ground. 'I'd rather not have anything to do with Portallen any more. I'll leave. Goodbye.'

'Oh, Cavan,' she moaned miserably.

'Do you want to know why I fixed it so we could appear to be engaged?' he asked curtly. 'Because I wanted to create the situation where we became lovers in private as well as public. I apologise that I misjudged your feelings. I honestly didn't think you had been in love with Dan. I didn't know you missed him so desperately.'

Cavan spun on his heel and walked from the room. Her mind seemed to be frozen. She heard him stumble along the corridor, heard the front door bang, heard him walking across the courtyard.

And then she realised she couldn't let him leave forever without telling him the truth about herself and Dan. There had been misunderstandings in the past because people had kept back their true feelings—the villagers who had been in awe of Cavan's physical prowess and grit and had never thought to tell him, her father who had loved Cavan and had desperately tried to keep his youthful exuberance in check, Rosie who had loved everyone and never thought to tell her own son that she loved him specially. Those misunderstandings had made Cavan wary of love, and she didn't want him never to experience its pain and its pleasures.

No more lies. No more pretences. Bethany felt her heart wrench with the poignancy of it all. If she had been given the chance to admire Cavan's flat and his achievements, they might have mellowed towards one another. He might not have become so passionately determined to dominate her sexually.

She gave a long moan and leapt up, dressing hastily and flying out of the house. Still shoeless, she stood on the cold stone step outside and frantically searched the darkness.

'Cavan! Cavan! Where are you?' she yelled.

She listened, but could only hear the roar of the sea on the shore. Heedless of her last pair of stockings, she raced down to the harbour, hoping to stop him before he reached the dinghy and returned to his yacht.

Breathless, hopeful, she flew along the sand. 'Cavan, Cavan, please *be there*, oh, Cavan!'

Something dark by the water stirred, and then she saw the blur of a shirt front. Sobbing, she flung herself at the figure, huddling in the welcoming arms, mumbling her relief in a muffled voice into the soft cloth of his jacket.

He thrust her from him. 'What are you saying? What are you *saying*, Bethany?' he demanded fiercely.

'Oh, Cavan!' she laughed hysterically. 'You have to know about me! I don't want you to go without knowing! I was very fond of Dan and we had some good times together but——'

He froze, but it was the stillness of expectancy. 'But?' he prompted gently when she hesitated.

Her face lifted to his. 'I feel so guilty,' she confessed. 'I wasn't everything I could have been to him. He adored me, but he knew that I had married him as second best. I didn't *know* that then because I was in a muddle about life and I had no idea what love really is—that it's hopeless and wonderful and warm as summer sea, and you don't care what happens to you so long as the person you love is happy.' She smiled dreamily. 'And you need him so much it's terrifying and you can't live without him . . . and life is miserable when you're not around and I can't bear to think of you going——'

A hard, ruthless mouth had possessed hers. She sank contentedly into the kiss, and was disappointed when it ended, knowing it must be their last. Her mouth had reached out to his, demanding more, but he had eased back from her, his eyes amused. She tensed and waited for his parting mockery because she'd wanted him to go on kissing her.

'I think you've given away a piece of unintended information. You said "life is miserable when *you're* not around". You "can't bear to think of *you* going". Does that mean me?' asked Cavan cautiously.

Her eyes widened in dismay. 'I said that? Did I?'

'Freudian slip,' he said huskily. 'Or I hope so.' His hand stroked her hot cheek. 'You were talking about love as if you really knew what it meant. Bethany,' he murmured, 'your heart is thudding so violently it's going to leap from your body. And I'm reading your eyes and discovering your secret. I was right. My instincts told me you cared for me, my brain said you didn't. You do, don't you?'

She avoided his eyes. 'I—I——'

He kissed her tenderly, and she tried not to enjoy it but her lips began to savour his hungrily and their passion deepened. 'You do care for me,' he said. She didn't answer, and he continued with the kiss. 'I'll go on doing this,' he told her huskily, 'till you answer truthfully.'

Her body tingled. Their mouths were welded together and the flames cruelly ate into her, destroying her resistance. His mouth lifted from hers, but his tongue flickered out, lightly running over the high arch of her lips, and she flung her head back in a helpless gesture.

'Tell me,' he insisted. His hands smoothed over her hips. She was finding it hard to breathe and her eyes were too drowsy to keep open.

'Tormenting...' she mumbled.

'Tell me.'

'All right!' she moaned. He immediately stayed his unfair assault. 'What's the use of denying it?' she said hopelessly. 'I fell head over heels for you when you first arrived. It was infatuation then. I fought it like mad. But...' She shrugged.

'Dear God!' he muttered. 'If Dan was second best, why on earth didn't you wait instead of rushing off to marry him?'

Bethany smiled faintly. 'What was the point? Whenever I tried to flirt with you, you scowled and walked off. I knew you would never settle in our little village, or look twice at an ordinary girl like me. You were so thrilled with your smart life in London. The receptionist,' she added ruefully, 'was equally thrilled with *you.*'

'Sweetheart, ever since I started shaving, women have been claiming all kinds of things where I'm concerned,' he said gently. 'I brought her down to Portallen because she said she wanted a job in a small country hotel to get over a boyfriend. It wasn't till we arrived that I realised she'd hoped I'd help physically to wipe away a few memories for her. I didn't make love to her. I was too wrapped up in my passion for you, and resisting it like hell. You were young and too close to home to play around with.'

'You hid your desire well,' she said ruefully.

He smiled. 'I had to. I knew what fire there was in you. I wanted to make my way in the world, and didn't want to get tied up with emotional entanglements before I'd made my fortune. So I convinced myself I was a rover, and fell in love twice a week like clockwork.'

He bent his head and kissed her, and they clung to one another for what seemed like an eternity. 'I think I ought to go home,' she breathed in his ear.

'No,' he growled. A quiver shook his body, and her eyes widened that he should want her so much. He hesitated. 'You must believe me when I tell you that Tania and I aren't lovers,' he said soberly, 'any more than that receptionist was.'

'I believe you,' she told him. 'I trust you.'

Before she knew what was happening, he had drawn her down to the hard, flat sand, kissing her with an urgency that left her breathless. Her body, already pushed to its limits, began to surrender, and her mind was weakened by her confession, which had swept away the barriers she'd built up against Cavan.

There, on the beach, with the sea roaring in her ears a few feet away, Cavan gently removed her clothes and then his, laying them beneath her willing body. The air was cold but she was filled with a madness, a hungry heat in her body that had been burning for so long that it desperately needed the long, slow plunge into the unknown depths with Cavan.

The world swirled around her, his hands and lips like silken water running over her body. They twined together, aching, longing, loving, the darkness of the night and the pounding of the surging tide on the rocks near by serving as a cloak of privacy.

His tenderness was shattering. Gently, persistently, he aroused her till she cried for release, and when it came it was in a long, shuddering sequence of ecstasy that drove her to the limits of pleasure till her ears thundered with it and the whole of her existence seemed to be focused in that one place.

'I love you,' she whispered. 'I love you.'

'Beth.' Cavan's voice came from a long way off, rich and deep and very, very satisfied.

'Mmm.' She couldn't move. Didn't want to. He loved her and she loved him and they'd just sealed that bond.

'I know this isn't romantic, but my feet are getting wet, sweetheart.'

'Mmm.' Then she gasped. A trickle of water had run along her naked thighs. Her eyes opened, and she saw Cavan propping himself up over her, his eyes laughing at her.

'Is this *Jaws II* or *From Here to Eternity*?' he murmured, as the tide lifted her body and gently pushed it up the beach.

She began to scramble up, laughing, her face flushed with shame at her total abandonment. 'I hope it's the latter,' she cried, shivering. 'Oh, my clothes!'

Cavan quickly caught them up, but it was too late. They were soaked. 'My plans didn't get this far,' he said helplessly. Bethany shivered again, and he opened his arms to her and he cuddled her, rubbing her back to keep her warm. 'My darling,' he murmured. 'I'll remember this for the rest of my life.'

She felt a pain in her heart. That sounded as if he was going to take the memory away with him—and not see her again. He'd got what he'd wanted. She tried to be matter-of-fact. 'This is so embarrassing! What are we going to do?' she whispered, peering around. 'Supposing anyone sees us on the way back? I'm freezing,

Cavan, think of something!' She saw the light in his eyes, and slapped his chest reprovingly. 'Greedy,' she reproved.

'Perhaps a little further up the beach?' he suggested huskily.

'Oh, lord,' she mumbled, trying not to enjoy his roaming hands. Her body arched into his. 'We *were* going home,' she reminded him.

'I found it impossible to wait,' he confessed. Water swirled around their ankles. 'We could slip around the beach to the dinghy and sneak out to the yacht,' he suggested. 'Unless Tania's taken the dinghy and is there already, in which case we'd have to borrow another boat to take us out.'

'I don't go in for threesomes,' she said tartly.

'Sweetheart, she's got her own cabin, thank God. We could use the double. Well, come on, Beth, it's all I can think of. Yes or no?'

'I can't...' She bit her lip. It would be wonderful to lie in the same bed as Cavan, but... 'Cavan, I can't... I think I'll put on my wet things and make a dash for it,' she mumbled. 'The idea of being in the same bed as you while Tania sleeps next door is too much.' With great difficulty she shook out her wet things and began to wriggle into them.

'I wasn't expecting to sleep,' admitted Cavan. 'Still, I tend to agree. You respond so very *noisily*.' Laughing at her blushes, he slipped on his jacket and, with a look of distaste on his face, yanked on his trousers, bundling the rest of their clothes into his shirt. 'Come on,' he chuckled. 'This is quite an adventure, sneaking home half naked! I feel like a teenager!'

'I think I'd rather not know what you got up to as a young man,' she said drily.

'I'll show you what I learnt when we get back,' he promised.

'I thought——'

'What did you think?' he asked gently. 'That I'd take you and leave you? That I'd taste paradise and turn my back on it? I'm not that disciplined, Bethany. Come here. I'll show you what I intend to do.'

They spent a blissful night together, making love, loving. Cavan was tender, passionate, fiery, impatient... Bethany could hardly believe that she could have felt so incredibly happy and utterly content, and she began to hope that the relationship would last.

Ignoring her protests in the morning that the workmen were arriving, he coaxed her into the bath, where he gently soaped her body, and then his hands became more urgent, his voice huskier and he had hauled her out on to the carpet, his fierce need for her melting her resistance. After, they lay dazedly in one another's arms till he finally rose and dried her.

'I'm crazy about you, Bethany,' he muttered into her thigh.

'I think I have proof of that,' she smiled contentedly. Her whole body sang and tingled. If this was the extent of Cavan's ability to love a woman, it was more than enough for her. She felt warm and very much adored. Bethany heaved a long sigh. 'I can hear noises in the kitchen. I suppose the workmen are having their tea before they start work.'

'Sweetheart,' laughed Cavan, leaving the bathroom to find his clothes, 'that's coffee they'll be making. It's gone eleven o'clock.'

'Oh!' She sat up quickly and ran in to the bedroom to dress as well. 'What will they think?' she cried, aghast.

'Look 'em in the eye and defy them to snigger,' Cavan advised drily. 'Though they'll have a job, if you go down with your jumper on inside out.'

She blushed at her fumbling, inept attempt at dressing. 'I seem to be all fingers and thumbs.'

He kissed them. 'And I can still feel their pressure all over my body,' he husked.

'Please, Cavan,' she said shyly.

'You are embarrassed, aren't you?' he remarked gently. 'Come on. Hide behind me.'

Bethany felt the eyes of the men must be boring into her when they entered the kitchen. But, before she could lift her head and answer their greetings, Cavan had stiffened in front of her. When he shifted slightly to one side, she saw that Tania was sitting at the kitchen table, a hard expression on her face.

'Well! You two look as if you've kissed and made up,' she said nastily.

'We have. Glad you realise that,' answered Cavan, not in the least put out.

Bethany accepted a mug of coffee from one of the men, her face rosy red. Tania looked sensational in a long white skinny-rib jumper and white wool tights, no skirt, but with high red boots. The workmen were mesmerised by her. Cavan, extraordinarily, didn't seem to notice anything unusual about Tania at all. He was busy raiding the fridge for bacon and eggs.

'You're very tolerant,' Tania said to Bethany. 'I'm damned if I'd forgive him for——'

'This is not the place to discuss what happened,' broke in Cavan. 'Besides, its no one's business but ours, so keep your dainty little nose out, Tania.'

Her dainty little nose wrinkled insolently. 'Darling,' she cooed to Cavan, 'in the excitement of the chase and the thrill of a successful kill, I think you've forgotten something. A teensy little trip you and I are supposed to be making together.'

'Oh, hell,' he frowned. 'The Brittany-Paris trip. You're right. I had.'

Bethany let Tania's implied taunts about Cavan's conquest go over her head. She was too disappointed that he was leaving to worry about Tania's bitchiness. 'I'd forgotten you were going away,' she said in dismay.

He glanced at his watch. 'I'll have to take breakfast on the run. I'd totally forgotten too, sweetheart. I ought to have left a couple of hours ago.'

'Can't Tania go on her own?' suggested Bethany, suddenly possessive. 'We've only just——' She stopped with a flurry of blushes colouring her face, aware that everyone was listening, fascinated.

'I can't get out of it. There has to be two of us,' he said with regret. Cavan took her hand and kissed her fingertips. 'It's too big an operation for me to miss it. I'd ask you to come, but I'm afraid——'

'Three's a crowd,' husked Tania, giggling.

'Don't be stupid,' scathed Cavan, kissing Bethany's cold lips. 'Darling, she's joking. This is business. Trust me. You have to, I'm afraid. Get used to this because I'll often go on these ticket "do"s. Our reunion alone with be worth it. Smile.'

She smiled. Falteringly. He was coming back to her, then. 'When will I see you again?' she asked, her face very wistful.

'Before you can get those curtains up in the drawing-room,' he assured her. 'In four days, five at the most.'

'There's Hawaii next,' drawled Tania. 'A week in the tropical paradise——'

'You can do that,' frowned Cavan.

'No, I can't, darling,' she said smugly. 'I'm on holiday. Remember?'

'Damn!'

'Could I go with you?' asked Bethany hesitantly.

Cavan took her in his arms. 'Time your coffee-break was over?' he suggested to the workmen. They took the hint. Cavan tenderly kissed Bethany. 'I can't let you come. Every second of every day is mapped out. It'll be awful. Totally exhausting. I'll be back in twelve days' time, then,' he said regretfully. 'I might not be very good company to begin with. I won't have had any sleep for two or three days.'

'*Naughty*,' murmured Tania.

'Find something to do in the coal cellar, will you?' suggested Cavan irritably. 'I want to say goodbye to Bethany, and the way I'm going to say it is not for your eyes or ears.'

'Don't be long,' said Tania, sounding spiteful. 'You'll need all your strength for this trip with me.'

She flung out of the room before Cavan could catch her with his outstretched arm. Heaving a sigh, he kissed Bethany again. 'I think that woman's got to go,' he muttered. 'She's too jealous of you.'

'Is she a good secretary, really?' asked Bethany unhappily.

'Terrific. I could shift her job sideways,' he mused. 'Give her responsibility, say...in Toronto. Hey! I'm wasting kissing time!'

Bethany surrendered to his passionate embrace. But in the back of her mind was a small, nagging doubt. When she waved him goodbye and watched him leave in the dinghy, she saw how close Tania stood by him, and that small, nagging doubt niggled in her mind, telling her that Cavan was highly sexed and Tania wanted him, and that anything could happen between a man and a woman at night on a boat.

CHAPTER EIGHT

HOWEVER, despite Bethany's worries, Cavan rang her every night, sounding adoring and loving. Hearing his voice was wonderful, and left her in a state of blissful happiness afterwards. Mawgan was delighted with her news, and teased her relentlessly. Cavan began to ring her during the day, too, and she gently rebuked him for wasting his money, but he only laughed and teased her, saying he was checking up on her in case she had slipped off with the electrician somewhere.

Then the calls stopped. She tried not to mind, to remember that he didn't belong to her in any way and was a free agent. It was hard, and for three days she worried—partly for Cavan, partly for herself. After all, he'd said that he had wanted to make love to her because it would relieve his obsession. Perhaps he'd got over her now, and he and Tania were laughing at her willingness to surrender herself to his demands.

Sitting in the kitchen, half-heartedly listening to the radio with its warnings of southerly gales one morning, she thought that it was sad that the house was becoming more beautiful every day as she was growing unhappier. Bethany glared at the postcard on the dresser which had been sent by Tania. From Hawaii.

'See your planning application's in,' commented the tiler, working around the sink unit.

She reached for the local paper he'd indicated eagerly. 'Did you say planning application? At last,' she said, turning to the page. 'Oh, yes. Here it is.' Her eyes widened as she read it. 'What? Application to convert hotel at Portallen Bay to a private residence? Private?' Bethany sat back in the chair in astonishment. *Private?*

Grimly she reached for the phone and dialled Mawgan's number, grateful that the tiler had politely left the room. Mawgan was amazed at her news.

'God, Beth, he's not trying to sell Portallen after all the work you've done, is he?' Mawgan exclaimed.

'I don't understand,' she said dully, a terrible fear shaping in her mind. 'Mawgan, you don't think he deliberately...that he... Oh, God!' she wailed.

'What is it?' cried her brother urgently.

'It's occurred to me that he only m-made love to me to keep me quiet, so that I'd go on renovating this place without charging him a penny.'

'I don't see why he should be so foul.'

'He said once I'd ruined his life,' she said in a flat tone. 'I did think at one time he'd written those poison-pen letters, remember. I could have been right. If so, he must hate me. This would be an amusing revenge, wouldn't it? I put my heart and soul into the Portallen Inn and he sells it at top-of-the-market rates. It would be a very neat kick in the teeth. He knows how much I love it.'

'But you said he'd rung you daily,' objected Mawgan, 'and been very affectionate.'

Her eyes closed in misery. 'How can I believe anything he says now? He deceived me about the Inn for ages. No wonder he wouldn't let me see the plans, or the proposed application,' she rasped. 'He'd decided on this from the start, I'm sure. There's something else, Mawgan. I didn't tell you, but Tania's sent me a postcard from Hawaii, and they both pretended she wasn't going to be with him.'

'Is that the problem? Don't worry,' he said comfortingly. 'I expect he needed her to do some work for him.'

'I do worry!' cried Bethany. 'She says they're having parties all night and that she's exhausting poor darling Cavan. She says he has a gorgeous tan and——' her voice shook slightly '—and that his white bit is startling,' she finished in a harsh voice.

'She's only trying her damnedest to make you jealous——'

'And succeeding,' muttered Bethany. 'That kind of information would shake any girl's confidence. I don't trust Tania. She'd do anything, say anything, I'm afraid, to get him. She said as much to me. Oh, Mawgan, she could have run to him with some story about me——'

'Boss is back.' The tiler's grinning face appeared in the doorway.

'I must ring off,' cried Bethany, her heart pounding. 'Cavan's here.'

'See, I told you,' laughed Mawgan. 'Brace yourself for a reconciliation scene.'

'Silly,' she smiled, her lips still trembling.

But she was nervous. When she reached the front door, there was no car to be seen, and she was about to go back and ask the tiler what he'd meant when she saw the yacht, bobbing in the choppy bay. Her heart stilled and became peaceful. She'd been wrong to suspect him. He'd come back to her. She leaned against the stone wall, waiting for the dinghy to come ashore, the strong wind whipping her hair into tangles.

After five minutes had passed, she felt cold so she slipped inside to put on a warm jacket, and then, on an impulse, she ran down to the quay.

'Jory, take me to Cavan's yacht, would you?' she cried urgently.

'OK. Don't be long out there,' he said, watching the scudding clouds. 'He'll need to run for shelter soon. We're too exposed here for him to stay anchored in the bay.'

Bethany nodded. A strange feeling welled up inside her and she pushed it aside. He'd be battening down hatches and preparing to leave, she told herself. That's why he didn't leap into the dinghy and make for shore. He was intending to shelter in the safety of Plymouth harbour and ring her from the yacht or take a taxi to Portallen for their reunion.

Her sense of foreboding increased as she approached the yacht. No one was on deck and there were no signs of life. She called but there was no reply. With difficulty, because of the windy conditions and the rising swell, Jory helped her on to the ladder and she clambered on board.

'Go back,' she called to him, shouting above the wind. 'I'll go out to sea with Cavan when he leaves the bay. It'll save time.' The boat lurched, and she grabbed the rail then scrambled over to the hatch. When she climbed down the steps into the big cabin she saw the remains of a meal, an empty bottle of wine on a cushion, two glasses in the sink, two plates, two...

'Cavan?' she called nervously. To her horror, Bethany heard a sound, a woman's voice. Her body became motionless while she listened, wondering what to do. If she didn't face up to this, she thought, she'd never know the truth.

The polished mahogany door opened to reveal Tania, in a flimsy baby-doll nightie. 'Beth!' cried Tania in genuine surprise. Mockingly she leaned against the bulkhead, a sultry expression on her face. 'I don't think you ought to go in there,' she said, indicating the cabin behind her. She smoothed her hands down her curvaceous body. 'Better be ignorant of what's been going on.'

'Cavan's in there?' whispered Bethany. 'Is that his cabin?'

Tania shrugged. 'His, ours, it's all the same.'

Bethany couldn't bring herself to go in. 'Where's the single cabin, then?' she asked tightly.

'Behind you.'

Spinning on her heel, Bethany pushed open the smaller door. The cabin contained a single bunk which was made up neatly. No one had slept in it that night. That was evidence enough for her. 'How long has this been going on?' she asked in a hard tone, stemming her longing to cry. 'You and him?'

'Since I started working for him and he took me on his knee in his office,' said Tania jauntily.

Bethany dropped her eyes, feeling sick. 'The classic boss and secretary situation! He won't get away with this,' she grated.

Suddenly she pushed past Tania into the room. Cavan lay on his stomach, his face to one side, cradled against the satin pillow. He was fast asleep—as heavily asleep as the day he'd crashed out in her bedroom. The upper part of his body was glistening with sweat as if he and Tania had been making passionate love. Tania came in behind Bethany, chuckling.

'Seen enough? He's quite dead to the world, poor darling. Handsome devil, isn't he? Sexy and rich as well. What more could a girl want?'

Bethany's contemptuous eyes blazed down on Cavan, the infamous oyster-coloured sheets rumpled in shimmering folds over his obviously naked hips. 'Cavan!' she said sharply.

'Don't wake him!' Tania's hand curled around Bethany's arm, but Bethany shook the red talons off with a violent gesture.

Cavan stirred and opened bleary eyes. 'My head!' he groaned, closing his eyes again. Tania ran over to sit on the bed and stroked his brow with a wet towel which was on a small table. A stab of anguish scorched through

Bethany's body. 'Mmm. More of that,' muttered Cavan in appreciation. 'What a night.'

'You miserable two-timing, conceited, badly bred gutter-snipe!' seethed Bethany.

'Whaat?' Cavan rolled over, and pushed himself up on his elbows. 'Beth...Bethany?' His eyes looked glazed as if he could hardly see her. He passed a shaking hand through his tousled hair, and she noticed that his voice was slurred.

'Drink is no excuse for what you've done,' she said sharply. 'Thanks, Tania. I'm grateful. I suppose if it hadn't been you, it would have been some other woman.'

'What—what's she saying?' frowned Cavan.

Tania smiled and dabbed at his forehead with the towel. 'Never mind, darling,' she crooned, stroking his back with her other hand. 'She's found out about us so we might as well own up.'

'I don't know how I could have been so blind,' said Bethany with quiet rage. 'You tricked me, I know. Lied like a trooper to get what you wanted. Well, you're welcome to each other. One of you is a man-eater, the other a common shark. And like all sharks you have to keep swimming in all the seas of the world to stay afloat, taking what you can, where you can with total disregard for the destruction that's left behind.' She tossed her dark head. 'Take Portallen,' she cried. 'Do whatever you want with it. I wash my hands of the place!'

He seemed stunned. 'Darling, give me a moment...I can't—you——'

'Don't you "darling" me! I'm walking out of Portallen, never to return. I leave you to pick up the pieces. Find yourself another fool to do all the hard work on that hotel free of charge.'

Cavan struggled to sit up, and every fumbling movement he made sliced into her with an agonising pain. He'd made love to Tania in the car and made love to *her* on the beach. He certainly had stamina. He'd lived it up in Hawaii, made passionate love to Tania after an alcoholic evening, and now he was suffering the consequences. She despised him, and was disgusted by the way he'd sated his lust with such crude thoroughness.

'You can't leave Portallen. You love it!' husked Cavan.

'I do!' she said angrily. 'That's the pity of it! But I'd rather go than finish the work and see it looking as I've always dreamed it would——'

'No, Beth, you mustn't go, you mustn't leave the job half done,' mumbled Cavan almost incoherently.

'You drunken swine! I can't live on thin air,' she snapped.

'You've got money,' said Tania sourly. 'You've got enough to buy yourself any man you want.'

'Me? That's a laugh! I haven't got a penny,' retorted Bethany recklessly. Her eyes glittered like striking flints. 'Who do you think bought the lifeboat?'

Tania flinched, her fingers lifting from where she'd been stroking Cavan's broad, naked shoulders. 'You?'

'Yes,' said Bethany, grim-faced. 'Every penny I had went into it.'

'Oh, no! You gave all your...' Tania gave a mirthless laugh. 'I don't believe you.'

'I can produce the receipt,' said Bethany coldly.

'You have no money?' frowned Cavan, holding his head as if it ached.

'None. I'm broke.'

Tania gave a low moan. 'Bethany! You—oh, my God! All this time I've been——' She bit her lip hard, her eyes troubled. 'You spent every penny of your compensation?' she asked.

'For the lifeboat,' said Bethany quietly.

'No, no! It saved my father,' cried Tania. 'Without it, he'd be dead.' Her mouth quivered and then she let out a wail. 'Oh, Beth!' To Bethany's astonishment, Tania ran to her and flung her arms around her, sobbing hysterically. 'I'm sorry, I'm so very sorry,' she cried. 'I didn't know you'd done that. I wouldn't have hurt you if I'd known. But you had everything: money, boys, looks, and Cavan.' Tania dropped her arms from around Bethany's waist and pulled away. 'I have something to tell you. Something awful and it's tearing my insides out. I wrote those poison-pen letters. I'm sorry. I know you'll never forgive me, but I was so desperately unhappy when you came back to Portallen looking so beautiful and——'

'You bitch, Tania! Get off this boat,' hissed Cavan, shakily wrapping a sheet around his waist, 'before I tear you limb from limb.'

Tania took one look at the malevolent glare on Cavan's face, the broad, powerful shoulders, the menacing way he was forcing his exhausted body from the bed, and scrambled back into the living quarters. 'I'm going, I'm going,' she moaned, climbing into a set of oilskins. She ran up the steps on to the deck, crying all the time.

Bethany couldn't move at all. Her mind whirled. It had been Tania, her old friend and confidante. Now everything fitted into place. She heard the outboard engine start up, and glanced at Cavan sympathetically. He'd made love to a spiteful, vicious and yet unhappy and unfulfilled woman who'd stopped at nothing to get him in her clutches.

Cavan had fallen back to the bed, breathing heavily, apparently still too dazed and drunk to stay upright for long. 'I feel terrible,' he muttered. 'Please find some ice.'

'I'll make some black coffee,' she said coldly. If he was to get his boat away before the gale struck with full force, he needed to be sober first. Her heart sank. Tania had taken the dinghy. She was stuck with Cavan.

She managed to brew the coffee with some difficulty. By the way the boat lurched and wallowed, it seemed the wind had increased in strength. When she got back to the cabin with a pot of coffee, she found that Cavan had dressed and was hanging on to the bulkhead, looking rather pale. The sweat still shone on his skin.

'Check on the weather,' he rasped through cracked lips.

Giving him a puzzled look, she slid the coffee-jug and his mug into the stabilising stand. He was terribly ill-looking. 'Drink all that,' she said sternly.

She heard rain begin to beat down on deck, and grabbed some oilskins. On deck, she could see the swell had increased—a sure sign of bad weather out to sea. The gale warning on the radio earlier had mentioned force eight to nine. Jory had been right; they couldn't stay in the harbour. No one wanted to be on a lee shore with weather like that approaching. They'd be safer if they stood off, or beat it to Plymouth.

Hastily she tumbled down the steps into the cabin. 'Hang on,' she told Cavan. 'It's going to be a bumpy ride. We're motoring out to sea.'

'Right,' he said hoarsely. 'I'll come up.'

'I have painful proof of your legendary stamina,' she snapped sarcastically, 'but you don't look as if you could handle a cuddly kitten let alone a yacht in a strong wind.'

But he joined her nevertheless, as she turned the nose of the boat into the wind and forged out to sea. Glancing quickly over her shoulder, she searched the bay to see if Tania was safe, and saw to her relief that the orange oilskinned figure was being helped ashore by Jory.

'Is Tania all right?' asked Cavan, concentrating on keeping his balance.

Bethany's mouth compressed into a hard line. 'She's a survivor,' she said crossly.

A sheet of rain, as fierce as hail, tipped from the leaden sky. Bethany could hardly see anything. Cavan switched on the radar and came up behind her, holding the bucking wheel with her. It was a nightmare journey. She forgot everything but the need to get through the gale and into Plymouth Sound. At last the bulk of the break-water came into sight and then Drake's Island. They hove to, and stood shaking for a while, cold, wet, exhausted.

Without speaking, they went below, shed their oil-skins and drank mugs of hot soup, then Bethany went to the single cabin and shut the door, flinging herself on the bed and sleeping fitfully.

The rocking of the boat grew less violent, and she eventually rose and went into the living quarters. To her alarm, Cavan was sprawled on the floor as if he'd been there all the time, his body saturated in sweat.

'What's the matter?' she asked anxiously when his eyes opened blearily.

'I'm sick. Food poisoning. Was getting over it,' he whispered, leaning his head back weakly. 'Pills.'

She ran into the cabin and found them, watching him while he swallowed one. His eyes closed. He fell asleep.

Bethany dragged him into the bedroom, inch by heavy inch. Unable to lift him on to the bed, she hauled all the blankets out of the locker and covered him up, then wet the towel to mop his brow. She paused. Tania had been doing that. Cavan had been ill even then.

Dismissing pity, she cooled his head and chest down and then tucked him up. And left him. He'd been Tania's lover. He should have stuck to one woman, not shared himself out. What had he said? Something about the need to master her because he'd never be satisfied if he didn't, like never managing to master backhand in tennis. Angrily she dumped the wine in the bin and began to clear up. It took a long time. Tania hadn't touched anything, and there were the remains of several meals lying around.

'Beth?'

It was a couple of hours later. Cavan had slept like a log, his heavy breathing vibrating through the boat. She'd been deliberately re-living his seduction so that she didn't weaken when he woke and tried to coax her to forgive him.

She turned. 'You look better,' she said evenly.

'I needed that sleep. The pill helped. I was taken ill in Hawaii,' he explained.

'I'm sure Tania was able to look after you. Was that why she abandoned her holiday, to look after you?' she asked with feigned interest.

Cavan gave her an odd look and began to pace up and down. 'It's like trying to dam the sea,' he muttered to himself. 'You build what you imagine to be something impregnable, and then all your efforts are wasted when a tiny little wave seeps in and undermines the foundations.'

'I don't see Tania Blake as a tiny little wave,' she said tartly.

'No,' he agreed morosely. 'She's as destructive as a tidal wave. Beth, I swear that we didn't make love——'

'Sorry, Cavan,' she said coolly. 'I'm past that kind of stupidity. I found her button in the car with a piece of material attached to it——'

'Then she tore it off herself,' he growled. 'Because I certainly didn't.'

'You were gone long enough,' Bethany said without emotion.

'I was trying to persuade her to lay off. I told her I wasn't interested——'

'I'm not stupid, Cavan! You lied when you said she wasn't going to Hawaii with you——'

'She turned up,' he protested irritably.

'Don't bother to make excuses. It's not worth the effort. I caught you both in bed together. It would take a woman of incredible denseness not to cotton on to the fact that you and she have been having an affair. Now I know for how long. Since she perched on your knee while you dictated to her,' she said bitterly, her calm manner vanishing.

'Don't be ridiculous. The only time she sat on my knee I pushed her off and she crashed to the floor,' he said grimly. 'How do you know she was in Hawaii?' he frowned.

'Postcard,' Bethany said succinctly, trying to control her anger. 'So don't flannel. She gave almost a detailed diary of your activities together.'

He groaned. 'I'll throttle the life out of her!' he muttered.

Bethany's eyes were the colour of the storm clouds outside. 'I don't take kindly to being two-timed. I despise you,' she scorned. 'All the time you were chatting to me on the phone and telling me you loved me, you were hot from Tania's arms, weren't you? My God! I'm going to make sure that you never set foot in Portallen again. I'll ruin your reputation——'

'Do that and I'll sue you for slander,' he frowned. 'I can prove I didn't have time to make love to her in Hawaii. Either my business partners or my clients were with me all the time. And they all know that I fell ill with severe food poisoning. I spent two days in the local hospital and then was invalided out on a stretcher. I have witnesses.'

'But you managed to have a romantic dinner for two on the yacht and then crawl into bed together after arriving in Portallen Bay,' she cried, unable to prevent herself from accusing him. 'I saw the wine, the plates— and I saw you both virtually naked in bed.'

'I remember nothing of a meal,' he said quietly. 'Tania must have eaten, I suppose. She never clears up after herself—it's usually me, but this time I was too ill and heavily sedated. Look, I don't even know how I got on to the boat. Tania must have organised everything for her own ends—my transfer to Plymouth airport, and I suppose on to the boat, though I didn't know where I was when you walked in on us. I was *ill*, Bethany!' he cried in exasperation. 'You must have seen.'

'I—I don't know...' She remembered the sweat on his body, his dazed look, and felt a little uncertain. 'I thought you were hung over.'

'You won't believe me, will you?' he asked in despair.

'You never tell me the truth,' she said unhappily. Her head lifted in defiance. 'Now wriggle out of the fact that you've changed your mind about Portallen! You intend it to be a house, don't you? A private house. That explains the design you approved, the alterations you insisted on. The single table. The——' she drew in her breath sharply '—the children's rooms on the top floor,' she grated. 'You bastard. You're going to sell it to some wealthy family. You never, ever intended it to be a hotel, did you?'

'No. Never,' he said bitterly. His eyes met hers and they were so full of pain that she felt an arrow shaft through her. 'Hadn't you realised?' he said wearily, seeing she didn't understand, and slumping to sit on the bed. 'It was to be your house.'

'Mine?' she scorned. 'Oh, that's clever——'

'Yes, I thought so,' he admitted. 'It was all done for you. I carefully found out your opinion on furniture, fittings, your likes, your dislikes, so that I could prepare it and make it absolutely what you wanted. It was for us,' he said moodily. 'What an arrogant, optimistic bastard I was! It was meant to be our future home. For you and me.'

Stunned, Bethany could only watch as he downed the rest of his tea. 'You and me? *Our* home?' she repeated stupidly.

'I have deceived you,' he conceded. 'But only for that end. I confess that I manipulated every situation. I made sure we got "engaged" so that we'd be thrown together. I wanted you to fall in love with me, and then I was going to present you with the house. Hoping, of course, that we'd marry and live in it together. But you won't believe me, you won't trust me and there's nothing I can do about that.'

'The nursery suite,' she repeated dully. 'That sweet little chair, the rocking horse——'

'God, Beth!' he groaned. 'Don't torture me! Isn't it enough that none of my dreams will come true? That I'll have to leave everything I've lovingly prepared for us and never see Portallen again, that I will never be able to touch, to see, to hold the woman I've wanted all my life? To see our children playing upstairs, learning to sail...? You've defeated me, Beth. I thought I could dominate you, override your objections to me, make you love me. It seems I can't.'

Bethany was still confused. What he was saying didn't tie up with his behaviour. 'I can't quite grasp what you're saying. Tania——'

'If she's got any sense, she'll be on her way to the airport. I told her she'd have to go to Toronto when she turned up in Hawaii and began to bat her eyelashes at me. I said I couldn't have a secretary who didn't give one hundred per cent of her working time to work. I've arranged it so that she's dumped on a friend of mine who's sixty-eight and happily married. She's lethal, Bethany. I'm beginning to realise how lethal.'

Suddenly, something occurred to Bethany. 'Cavan,' she said urgently, 'it was Tania who told me there was a call on your car-phone, the night of the harvest festival. That's when I found the button on the driver's seat.'

'Tania,' he breathed harshly. His eyes kindled. 'I won't throttle her. I'll bury her alive!' he said savagely.

Bethany's fingers touched his chest to stay his temper. 'No,' she said quietly. 'I know what it's like to be denied the man you're deeply in love with. She will be very unhappy. She deserves nothing else.'

'Oh, she'll soon be happy when she finds a Canadian millionaire,' Cavan said grimly. 'Any rich man between puberty and death will suit her. She's very shallow.' He inhaled harshly. 'Do you want me to get you ashore?' he asked with simulated indifference.

A slow beautiful smile broke over Bethany's face. She was beginning to register what Cavan had said, turning it over in her mind. He'd gone to an incredible amount of effort to create the home she desired. She looked at him with tenderness. 'You bought that expensive fireplace for us?' she asked in awe.

He scowled. 'Stupid, wasn't it?' he said with a self-mocking laugh. 'I was thrilled when you said you liked it.'

'The top floor. That was going to be for our children's bedrooms, a playroom and a nursery suite?' she asked breathlessly.

'Someone will buy it,' he said gruffly, turning his back on her.

She sat on the bed beside him and put her hand on his arm. 'Cavan,' she said gently. 'You say you've wanted me all your life and that you've wanted me to love you. But there's something you haven't told me yet. Something important.'

He kept his head low and averted, and she could only see his clenched jaw and the slight sheen on his face where the fever still lay within him. 'That I love you?' he asked hoarsely. 'That you are everything in life to me and without you I have no meaning and no purpose? Is that what you want to hear? Do you want to exact all your revenge on me, Bethany, because I fixed my love on you years ago and never wavered? All right,' he cried, facing her belligerently, 'so I love you! But how can you ever trust me?'

She smiled gently at him, and his hot despair melted away to be replaced by a growing realisation that she was looking at him with loving eyes. He'd gone to an enormous amount of trouble to please her. 'Cavan Trevelyan,' she murmured, reaching up to touch his chiselled mouth, 'for a street-wise ticket-tout, you're amazingly stupid.'

'I—I can hardly believe... You mean you're not angry? Oh, Beth, I do love you, passionately, so much that I'm afraid of hurting you,' he said fervently.

'I love you, Cavan,' she said softly.

He grinned in sudden, blinding delight, his eyes searching hers in amazement. 'You love me. You love me! We can live in Portallen? Fill the nursery with our children——?'

'Steady. I'm having a career first,' she said firmly. 'We have to use those twin-facing desks for a while, don't we?'

'You'll marry me?' he asked, still bemused. 'A jumped-up ticket-tout?'

'How else can I get tickets for the centre court at Wimbledon every year?' she laughed. Life was suddenly wonderful. Maybe she had a little way to go before she won over the villagers, but, with Cavan's help, she'd make it.

He growled sexily in his throat. 'I think,' murmured Cavan, drawing her down to the bed, his eyes adoring her, 'that I'm at last going to be able to perfect my backhand.' He kissed her and stroked her face. 'And my forehand.' He touched her parted lips and kissed her neck. His hand slid down to her thigh. 'And my serve,' he whispered.

Bethany's eyes began to close with desire. 'I have the feeling that this is going to be a very long match,' she husked as her body arched into his.

Cavan shuddered, his mouth devouring hers passionately while the boat rocked gently in the sheltering harbour, the gale blowing itself out down the coast. 'With only one score. Love all,' he breathed.

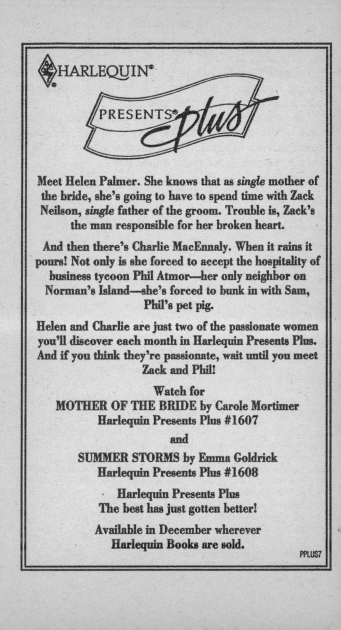

HARLEQUIN®

PRESENTS® *Plus*

Meet Helen Palmer. She knows that as *single* mother of the bride, she's going to have to spend time with Zack Neilson, *single* father of the groom. Trouble is, Zack's the man responsible for her broken heart.

And then there's Charlie MacEnnaly. When it rains it pours! Not only is she forced to accept the hospitality of business tycoon Phil Atmor—her only neighbor on Norman's Island—she's forced to bunk in with Sam, Phil's pet pig.

Helen and Charlie are just two of the passionate women you'll discover each month in Harlequin Presents Plus. And if you think they're passionate, wait until you meet Zack and Phil!

Watch for
MOTHER OF THE BRIDE by Carole Mortimer
Harlequin Presents Plus #1607

and

SUMMER STORMS by Emma Goldrick
Harlequin Presents Plus #1608

Harlequin Presents Plus
The best has just gotten better!

Available in December wherever
Harlequin Books are sold.

**Fifty red-blooded, white-hot, true-blue hunks
from every State in the Union!**

Look for MEN MADE IN AMERICA! Written by some
of our most poplar authors, these stories feature fifty of
the strongest, sexiest men, each from a different state in
the union!

Two titles available every other month at your favorite
retail outlet.

In November, look for:

STRAIGHT FROM THE HEART by Barbara Delinsky
(Connecticut)
AUTHOR'S CHOICE by Elizabeth August (Delaware)

In January, look for:

DREAM COME TRUE by Ann Major (Florida)
WAY OF THE WILLOW by Linda Shaw (Georgia)

You won't be able to resist MEN MADE IN AMERICA!